STAR WARS

THE

MANDALORIAN

SEASON 2

JUNIOR NOVEL

Adapted by Joe Schreiber

Based on the series created by Jon Favreau and written by
Jon Favreau, Dave Filoni, and Rick Famuyiwa

DISNEY
LUCASFILM
PRESS
Los Angeles • New York

For information address Disney • Lucasfilm Press,
1200 Grand Central Avenue, Glendale, California 91201.

Printed in the United States of America

First Edition, January 2022

1 3 5 7 9 10 8 6 4 2

FAC-025438-21323

ISBN 978-1-368-07596-1

Library of Congress Control Number on file

Visit the official *Star Wars* website at: www.starwars.com.

SUSTAINABLE
FORESTRY
INITIATIVE
Certified Chain of Custody
Promoting Sustainable Forestry
www.sfiprogram.org
SFI-01054
The SFI label applies to the text stock

A long time ago in a galaxy far,
far away. . . .

CHAPTER 01

THIS WAS NO PLACE for a child.

The Mandalorian made his way down the backstreet with the silver pram floating alongside him, its tiny occupant safely within reach. Inside, the Child sat wide-eyed, taking in his surroundings with a whimper. The slums of this Outer Rim planet were flooded with menacing shadows, every one of them threatening trouble. Rows of streetlights flickered overhead, casting their uncertain glow across the graffiti-strewn walls as if fearful of what they might find. The sweltering air around them was motionless and hushed, yet the quiet was deceptive.

They were not alone.

In the darkness, eyes gleamed.

Mando stopped in front of a darkened doorway where a Twi'lek guard stood with his arms crossed.

Like all of his kind, the Twi'lek was humanoid in most respects, with the exception of the two elongated lekku that protruded from his skull. His gaze was cold, an unspoken challenge to anyone unlucky enough to have found their way there by accident, as he waited for the Mandalorian to state his business.

"I'm here to see Gor Koresh," Mando said, and the Child cooed in agreement. After a moment, the doorman moved aside, gesturing them in.

"Enjoy the fights," the Twi'lek said.

Stepping inside, Mando could already hear cheers and applause, and the clang of metal on metal. In the ring, two massive, piglike Gamorrean fighters were battling each other with vibro-axes while the spectators whistled and roared in a half dozen different languages and dialects. Mando scarcely bothered to glance over, although the Child seemed fascinated by the display of brutality inside the ropes.

Surveying the crowd, Mando found the one he was looking for.

Gor Koresh was a green-skinned Abyssin with a flair for style, adorned in a spotless white suit, earrings, and nose ring. Four heavily armed bodyguards surrounded him, their attention riveted to Mando and his companion in the floating pram. Koresh's solitary eye moved from the Child to Mando with a mixture of bemusement and disapproval.

"You brought the kid?"

"Wherever I go," Mando said, "he goes."

Koresh snorted. "So I've heard."

"I have been quested to bring him to his kind," Mando said. "If I can locate other Mandalorians, they can help guide me. I'm told you know where to find them."

Koresh scarcely took his attention from the fighters. "It's uncouth to talk business immediately," he said. "Just enjoy the entertainment."

Entertainment wasn't the word Mando would've chosen to describe what was going on inside the ring, but he waited as the two fighters swung axes at each other, pounding their way through the final act of their sweaty, desperate drama. One of them caught his opponent with a blow to the midsection, knocking him to the mat, and the crowd roared.

"Bah!" Koresh grunted, clearly displeased by this outcome. "My Gamorrean is not doing well." He raised his voice to a shout, joining the jeers and cries of the mob. "Kill him! Finish him!"

As if in response to this command, the injured Gamorrean recovered his balance and launched a counterattack. Koresh jerked his head toward the bounty hunter.

"Do you gamble, Mando?"

"Not when it can be avoided," the Mandalorian said.

Koresh laughed unpleasantly. "I will bet you the information you seek that this Gamorrean is going to die within the next minute and a half. And all you have to put up in exchange is your shiny beskar armor."

Mando turned to look at him. "I'm prepared to pay you for the information," he said. "I am not leaving my fate up to chance."

"Nor am I," Koresh said. Inside the ropes, the winning fighter had raised his ax to finish off his opponent. Without hesitation, the cyclops rose to his feet, pulled a blaster from the shoulder holster beneath his suit jacket, aimed, and fired into the ring, hitting the standing Gamorrean squarely in the chest and knocking him off his feet, ending the fight.

As a shocked silence fell over the room, Koresh swung the blaster around on the Mandalorian. Before Mando could draw his own sidearm, the surrounding bodyguards had already responded, their weapons trained on the bounty hunter at point-blank range.

Around them, the crowd seemed to have suddenly lost all interest in bloodshed. They jumped from their seats and scrambled toward the exits, leaving Mando and the Child alone with Koresh and his thugs.

"Thank you for coming to me," Koresh said. "Normally I have to seek out remnants of you Mandalorians in your hidden hives to harvest your precious shiny shells." He chuckled again. "Beskar's value continues to rise. I have grown quite fond of it. Give it to me now, or I will peel it off your corpse."

The Mandalorian didn't move. Next to him, he could see the Child peering up from the edge of the pram, following the discussion with rapt attention.

"Tell me where the Mandalorians are," Mando said, "and I'll walk out of here without killing you."

Koresh's eyebrow tightened in a scowl. "I thought you said you weren't a gambler."

"I'm not," Mando said. Seeing what was coming, the Child ducked into the egg-shaped pram and snapped the shell closed just as Mando activated the brace of homing missiles in his wrist gauntlet. The whistling birds swept through the bodyguards in a deadly swarm, dropping all of them in a matter of seconds.

There was a howl of rage as the surviving Gamorrean gladiator vaulted over the ropes, plunging toward Mando. Mando stepped back, and the Gamorrean crashed to the floor with a bone-jarring thud. An instant later the bounty hunter felt a pair of arms grabbing him from behind as three more armed fighters in Koresh's employ charged him with an onslaught of punches and kicks. One of them swung a battle hammer, and Mando ducked in time to see Koresh dashing for the exit.

Mando smashed the Twi'lek in front of him with a fist to the skull, then pivoted and took out the thug behind him before ejecting a spring-loaded blade from his wrist and finishing off the last two fighters with lethal efficiency. He picked up his blaster and sprinted for the door in pursuit of the Abyssin.

Outside he found Koresh scurrying down the alleyway, elbows pumping, making little grunting noises of panic as he fled. The Mandalorian raised his arm and fired a grappling cable, snaring the cyclops around the ankles and yanking him off his feet, then dragging him backward. Mando looped the cable around a lamppost and hoisted Koresh into the air so he was hog-tied and dangling upside down, his soiled white jacket flapping around him like a pair of useless wings.

"All right!" Koresh said. "Stop! I'll tell you where he is. But you must give me your word that you won't kill me."

"I promise you won't die by my hand," Mando said. He could already hear the red-eyed creatures in the shadows creeping closer. Their claws made eager little scratching noises as they approached. "Now, where is the Mandalorian you know of?"

"Tatooine."

Mando looked at him in surprise. "What?"

"The Mando I know of is on Tatooine," Koresh said. Having already sacrificed all dignity, his voice cracked as he sought to preserve what remained of his composure.

"I have spent much time on Tatooine," Mando said. "I have never seen a Mandalorian there."

"My information is good, I tell you. The city of Mos Pelgo." The Abyssin's voice was starting to sound hoarse, as if he was struggling to breathe. "I swear it by the Gotra!"

"Tatooine it is then," Mando said, and turned to leave, the Child's pram floating alongside him.

"Wait, Mando!" Koresh cried. "You can't leave me like this! Cut me down!"

"That wasn't part of the deal."

Turning, the Mandalorian shot out the streetlight above Koresh. All around him, emboldened by the darkness, the red-eyed shapes lunged at their prey, and Gor Koresh began to scream. "Wait, what are you doing? Mando! I can pay! *Mando!*"

But the Mandalorian didn't look back.

CHAPTER 02

TATOOINE. It was like he'd never left.

Gliding high above its dunes and canyon vistas, Mando brought the *Razor Crest* over the sprawling golden sandscape, passing a Tusken Raider astride his bantha on a cliff overlooking Mos Eisley. He guided the ship downward, settling it into its now familiar berth in hangar three-five, then lowered the ramp in a cloud of hydraulic steam.

Peli Motto was waiting for him in her usual jumpsuit and tool belt, her droids already advancing like a pit crew toward the ship. She shooed them away.

"All right," she said. "Hey, hey, hey! Sorry, gang." She shook her head. "Come on, you know he doesn't like droids."

Mando walked down the ramp, a satchel hanging

from his shoulder. "You might as well let them have at it," he said. "The *Crest* needs a good once-over."

Peli Motto raised an eyebrow. "Oh? So he likes droids now? Well, you heard him. Give it the once-over." As the droids made their way toward the ship, Peli turned her attention to Mando. "I guess a lot has changed since you were last in—" Her voice rose in excitement as she noticed the Child's head peeking out of the bag. "Oh, thank the Force! This little thing has had me worried sick. Come here, you little womp rat." She scooped up the Child and chuckled as he cooed in her arms. "Looks like it remembers me." Then, glancing up at Mando: "How much do you want for it? Just kidding—but not really. You know, if this thing ever divides or buds, I will gladly pay for the offspring."

There was a whoosh and a crash from the *Razor Crest*, and she and Mando looked over to see a loose hydraulic hose flailing in the air. "Hey!" Peli shouted. "Watch what you're doing up there! He barely trusts your kind!"

Mando returned his attention to her. "I'm here on business," he said. "I need your help."

"Then business you shall have," Peli said, still

cradling the Child in her arms. "Care for me to watch this wrinkled critter while you seek out adventure?"

"I've been quested to bring this one back to its kind," Mando said.

"Oh, wow. I can't help you there. I've never seen any like it."

"A Mandalorian armorer has set me on my path," Mando said. "If I can locate another of my kind, I can chart a path through the network of coverts." He told her about Mos Pelgo and what he hoped to find there, and what he needed from her.

"You still have that speeder bike?"

"Sure do," Peli said. "It's a little rusty, but I got it."

Mando followed her out.

Peli was right: the bike *was* rusty, but it still managed to carry them across the dunes with plenty of speed and lift, Mando gripping the controls and the Child riding happily inside the saddlebag, ears flapping in the breeze. Even at high speed, the journey took them well into the shadows of dusk. They spent the night among an encampment of Tusken Raiders gathered with their banthas around a campfire, the Mandalorian making silent conversation with them through hand gestures and sign language, getting directions to go forward, as the Child feasted on roasted womp rat. In the morning they set out again, hoping to reach their destination before midday.

The town of Mos Pelgo was not much more than a windswept mining settlement made up of an assortment of raised structures and stilted storefronts. Some of the houses were made of baked clay, perched atop decking to keep them from sinking into the sand. The residents huddled in doorways, glaring in wary silence and outright suspicion as Mando rode down the street and then stopped to dismount in front of the saloon.

Inside the establishment seemed very dark after the brightness of the day, but Mando could see it was mostly empty. The Weequay behind the bar glanced up at him.

"Can I help you?"

"I'm looking for a Mandalorian," Mando said.

"Well, we don't get many visitors in these parts. Can you describe 'em?"

"Someone who looks like me."

The wrinkly-skinned bartender looked at him for another moment, wondering if he was being put on. "You mean the marshal?"

"Your marshal wears Mandalorian armor?"

"See for yourself," the bartender said, gesturing with a thrust of his chin.

Mando turned to look at the figure in the doorway, silhouetted against the bright desert sky. The man was indeed wearing beskar armor and a helmet.

"What brings you here, stranger?"

"I have been searching for you for many parsecs," Mando said.

"Well, now you've found me," the marshal said as he stepped inside, his boots creaking against the floorboards. "Weequay, two snorts of spotchka." He turned to Mando. "Why don't you join me for a drink?"

Without waiting for Mando's response, the marshal took the bottle of blue liquid and two glasses and carried them to a nearby table, where he sat down.

Then he did the last thing Mando would've expected: he took off his helmet.

"I've never met a real Mandalorian," the man said with a slight smile. He was tan and lean-featured, with a scruff of beard and a bemused glint in his eye. "Heard stories—I know you're good at killing. And probably none too happy to see me wearing this hardware. So I figure only one of us is walking out of here." He glanced over to where the Child stood peering into a spittoon.

"But then I see the little guy, I think maybe I pegged you wrong?"

"Who are you?" Mando asked.

"I'm Cobb Vanth," the man said. "Marshal of Mos Pelgo."

"Where did you get the armor?"

Vanth raised the glass to his mouth and sipped. "Bought it off some Jawas."

"Hand it over," Mando said.

"Look, pal," Vanth said, and put down the glass. "I'm sure you call the shots where you come from. But around here, I'm the one that tells folks what to do."

"Take it off." Mando took a step toward him. "Or I will."

Vanth didn't appear terribly intimidated by this threat. If anything, he seemed to welcome the inevitable confrontation with the air of a man dispatching with the formalities and getting down to business.

"We gonna do this in front of the kid?" he asked.

Over by the spittoon, the Child made a soft cooing sound. "He's seen worse," Mando said.

"Right here then?"

"Right here."

With a shrug, Vanth scraped back his chair and

rose to face the Mandalorian. His hand moved to the holster at his hip, fingers ready. Behind the bar, the Weequay stood motionless, holding his breath, as the Mandalorian waited for the marshal to make his move.

Then the earthquake started.

CHAPTER 03

THE TREMOR RATTLED the entire bar, clinking glassware and making the spittoon rock back and forth on the floor. Vanth held up one finger as if to say, *Hold it right there*, before turning and walking to the doorway. The rumbling had become more intense. In the distance, Mando heard a siren going off.

He stepped outside to join Vanth in front of the saloon. The marshal was staring down the main street, out into the distance. All around them, the residents of Mos Pelgo were shouting and running for their homes. An anxious bantha tethered to a nearby hitching post brayed in fear.

Something was coming.

It approached with a deafening roar. Mando could see the shape beneath the ground, its spiny ribs protruding from the sand, the vibration of its howl disrupting the soil, loosening it and making it shift and swirl like waves on an ocean. Then all at once the thing erupted into view, mouth gaping, even bigger than Mando had expected, like a living cave full of teeth. It rose up and closed over the bantha, devouring it in a single bite, before disappearing again beneath the surface in a spray of sand and grit.

Vanth and Mando stood on the porch in front of the saloon, watching the dust settle in the midday suns. Inside the drinking establishment, the Child poked his head out of the spittoon where he'd sought shelter. Finally, Cobb Vanth sighed.

"Maybe we can work something out," he said.

He and Mando walked along the raised platform that led away from the saloon. Around them, the citizens were already making repairs. There was something about the routine that made Mando think it had happened many times before, a common enough occurrence around the settlement.

"That creature has been terrorizing these parts long before Mos Pelgo was established," Vanth said. "Thanks to this armor, I've been able to protect this town from bandits and Sand People. They look to me to protect them. But a krayt dragon is too much for me to take on alone." He turned to Mando. "Help me kill it, I'll give you the armor."

"Deal," Mando said, the plan already taking shape in his mind. "I'll ride back to the ship, blow it out of the sand from the sky, use the banthas as bait."

"Not so simple," Vanth said. "A ship passes above, it senses the vibrations and stays underground. But I know where it lives."

"How far?" Mando asked.

The marshal's eyes flicked off to the distance. "Not far."

Together they set out into the desert. Mando took his speeder bike, and Vanth rode a modified podracer engine equipped with a saddle and flight controls as they jetted along the swells toward the Jundland Wastes.

"You don't understand what it was like," Vanth said, raising his voice to be heard above the podracer engine. "The town was on its last legs. It started after we got news of the Death Star blowing up. The second one, that is. . . ."

The marshal told Mando how the Empire had pulled out of Tatooine as the occupation ended. At first, there had been cheering in the streets—but the celebration hadn't lasted long. That very night, the Mining Collective had moved in. Armed soldiers hiding behind dark face visors had poured into the bar, brutally taking control and bringing the locals in line.

"Power hates a vacuum," Vanth said, "and Mos Pelgo became a slave camp overnight." He gazed off into the distance, reliving the memory in his mind. "I lit out, took what I could from the invaders. I grabbed a camtono. I had no idea it was full of silicax crystals." He described how he'd escaped from town and out into the desert, wandering for days without food or water, on the verge of collapse. "And then I was saved. By Jawas."

The desert scavengers had been fascinated with the silicax crystals that Vanth had unknowingly been carrying with him. They'd given him shelter aboard the sandcrawler, provided water and a chance to recover. "The Jawas were in awe of the crystals," Vanth said. "They wanted them at any cost, and offered their finest in exchange. My treasure bought me more than a full water skin. It bought my freedom."

The salvaged beskar armor that the Jawas had been carrying aboard the sandcrawler was badly pitted and pockmarked from the harsh desert environment they'd found it in, but even then, Vanth had seen its potential— not just for himself but for the salvation of Mos Pelgo.

He explained to Mando how he'd gone back to the settlement wearing the helmet and armor, having brought its long-dormant weapons systems back online.

The mining colony enforcers were still in the saloon, lounging at the tables. Vanth had pulled his blaster and opened fire, taking them out without getting a scratch. When the last of the enforcers had tried to flee in a landspeeder, Vanth stepped outside and launched a missile from his back, taking out the speeder before it could reach the open desert.

That was how he'd become the marshal of Mos Pelgo.

His story ended as they reached the canyons of the Jundland Wastes. It was eerily still as Vanth and Mando trawled slowly through the sandstone catacombs, sounds echoing around them. Movement flickered along a nearby ridge, and Mando saw a menacing pack of massiffs coming into view. The reptilian lizard-wolves growled at them, claws shuffling and clicking on the rocky sand.

Vanth raised his blaster and took aim, but Mando reached out and gently pushed his barrel down. Then Mando let out a guttural howl that echoed into the canyon. There was silence.

"What are you doing?" Vanth asked.

A moment later, a half dozen Sand People emerged from their cover. Mando set down his rifle and walked over. Two of the massiffs bounded toward him like over-size puppies, sniffing Mando curiously. As the Tusken Raiders started signing with him, Mando responded.

"Hey, partner," the marshal said. "You want to tell me what's going on?"

Mando squatted down and ran one hand roughly over a wolf-lizard's head, patting its chest.

"They want to kill the krayt dragon, too," he said.

That night they sat with the Tuskens around their camp-fire, their domed huts flickering in the firelight. One of the Sand People cracked open a black egg and passed it to Vanth, who scowled at the contents with undis-guised revulsion.

"What am I supposed to do with this?" he asked.

"You drink it," Mando said.

"It stinks."

"Do you want their help?"

"Not if I have to drink this," Vanth said.

The Tuskens argued with signing, and Mando replied with a series of gestures, then turned to Vanth. "He says your people steal their water, and now you insult them by not drinking it." He signed again with the Tusken. "They know about Mos Pelgo. They know how many Sand People you've killed."

"They raided our village," Vanth protested. "I defended the town!"

"Lower your voice."

Around them, the Sand People began to stir with aggression. The massiffs edged out of the shadows, stalking closer, growling.

"I knew this was a bad idea," Vanth said.

"You're agitating them," Mando told him. The Tuskens were rising, reaching for their weapons, and Vanth was already going for his blaster.

The marshal tossed the contents of the egg aside with a dismissive jerk of his hand. "These monsters can't be reasoned with," he said, and lunged to his feet, glaring at the Tusken nearest to him. "Sit down before I put a hole through you! I'm not going to say it—"

WHOOSH! A plume of flame erupted upward from Mando's wrist, disrupting the confrontation and forcing the Tuskens and Vanth to take a step back. In the ensuing silence, Mando howled out to the Sand People and signed furiously at them.

"What are you telling them?" Vanth demanded.

"The same thing I'm telling you," Mando said. "If we fight among ourselves, the monster will kill us all. Now"—he continued signing to the Tuskens—"how do we kill it?"

◆

They traveled by bantha, single file, deeper into the wastes. Mando rode one, with the Child secured in a saddlebag, and Cobb Vanth was astride another, not particularly pleased to have traded his modified pod-racer engine for the beast lumbering underneath him. He was probably wondering how he'd found himself riding alongside the people he'd always thought of as his enemies.

At last they reached a cliff overlooking the wastes, and a cave gaping among sandstone crags at the base of a rocky canyon. Mando watched as one of the Tuskens raised a pair of binoculars to survey the land. Mando recognized the binocs—they were the same pair the Sand People had taken from Toro Calican not so long before.

Down below them, one of the Tuskens made his way through the floodplain toward the mouth of the cave, leading a reluctant-looking bantha.

"They say it lives in there," Mando told Vanth. "They say it sleeps. It lives in an abandoned sarlacc pit."

The marshal shook his head. "I've lived on Tatooine

my whole life," he said. "There's no such thing as an abandoned sarlacc pit."

"There is if you eat the sarlacc."

They continued to watch as the Tusken outside the cave scattered some bantha food to preoccupy the bait. Next to them, the Sand People murmured among themselves, and the marshal waited for the bounty hunter to translate.

"They're laying out a bantha to protect their settlement," Mando said. "They've studied its digestion cycle for generations. They feed the dragon to make it sleep longer."

The Tusken below them tied the bantha to a post and began to shuffle away.

"Watch," Mando said. "The dragon will appear."

They didn't have to wait long. From the mouth of the cave, the thing burst forth with a deafening roar. Mouth gaping, it ignored the bantha offering and instead devoured the fleeing Tusken in a single bite before withdrawing back into the cave.

Mando glanced at Vanth. "They might be open to some new ideas," he said.

◆

Back at the Tusken camp, Mando and Vanth gathered with the Tuskens around a makeshift model of the krayt dragon made of womp rat bones. The Sand People huddled close, snorting and signing, as Mando and Vanth studied the battle plan.

"What are the bones?" the marshal asked.

"That's the dragon," Mando said.

"And those little rocks?"

"That's us."

Vanth shook his head. "It's not to scale."

"I think it is," Mando told him.

"It can't be," Vanth said. "That's too big."

Mando signed a question. The Tusken nodded.

"It's to scale," Mando said.

"I've only seen its head and neck," the marshal said. "That's a whole lot bigger than I guessed. Might be time to rethink our arrangement."

The Tuskens pointed at each other and began scattering more pebbles around the giant dragon.

"That's more like it," Vanth said. "Where are they getting the reinforcements?"

Mando decided to give him the news. "I volunteered your village," he said.

CHAPTER 04

THE NEWS DID not go over well.

Back at the saloon, the citizens of Mos Pelgo were already arguing with the marshal as he tried to explain the situation and how the Sand People would help them slay the dragon. Vanth had expected resistance, and the crowd did not disappoint him.

"They raid our mines!" someone protested.

"They're monsters," the Weequay bartender added.

Vanth was trying to figure out how to reply when Mando stepped forward. "I've seen the size of that thing," the bounty hunter said. "It will swallow your entire town when the fancy hits it. You're lucky Mos Pelgo isn't a sand field already."

The villagers fell silent. As painful as it was, the truth spoken bluntly by a stranger carried the undeniable ring of authority.

"I know these people," Mando continued. "They are brutal, but so is the Dune Sea. They have survived for thousands of years in these sands, and they know the krayt dragon better than anyone here." He paused to let that fact sink in. "They are raiders, it's true. But they also keep their word. We have struck a deal. If we are willing to leave them the carcass and its ichor, they will stand by our side in battle and vow never to raise a blaster against this town, until one of you breaks the peace."

The crowd looked at each other. There was a slow nodding of heads, a grim acknowledgment of what needed to be done. For better or worse, a partnership had been forged.

Cobb Vanth hoped they survived to enjoy it.

On the outskirts of town, humans and Sand People labored alongside one another in an uneasy alliance, passing crates of mining explosives and loading them onto the backs of banthas. When one of the explosives slipped from a Tusken's grasp, the man who'd handed it to him yelled angrily, "What are you trying to do, blow us all up?"

The Tusken responded with equal hostility, and Vanth stepped in to defuse the situation.

"It was an accident," Vanth said. When the man and

the Tusken moved back, each muttering to himself, the marshal turned to Mando. "It's gonna be great," he said, as if trying to convince them both.

Once the munitions were loaded, the group rode along the ridgeline into the Jundland Wastes, making their way back to the dragon's lair. At the mouth of the cave, one of the Sand People approached and knelt down, pressing one hand to the ground, then signed a message up to the rest.

"What'd he say?" Vanth asked.

"He says it's sleeping." The bounty hunter paused. "If we listen carefully, we can hear it breathing."

As they peered down, the Tusken next to the marshal drank from a black egg and passed it to him. Vanth glanced down at it, sighed, and took a drink.

"Let's get to work," Mando said.

"The Tuskens say the belly is the only weak spot," Mando said as the group worked together side by side to bury the explosive charges outside the cave. Other Tuskens stood farther out along the floodplain, assembling an array of what looked like oversize mechanical crossbows with barbed harpoons fastened to long coils of thick cable. "We have to wake it up and get it angry enough to charge. Once it's far enough out and the belly is above the explosives, you hit the detonator."

The rest of the plan came together quickly enough. A small group of Sand People approached the cave opening, their figures appearing tiny and vulnerable compared with the darkness that surrounded them.

Cobb Vanth and the Mandalorian watched from above. Outside the cave, one of the Tuskens sent an ear-piercing howl into the depths of the catacombs below and was met with a responding howl from inside the cave. Seconds later, the dragon burst forth, its jaws open, revealing rows of teeth the size of tombstones. The fleeing Tuskens were almost immediately overtaken by the yawning mouth.

From behind Vanth came a battle cry, and the tripod-mounted crossbows fired, harpoons flying forward and wedging into the hide of the dragon. The chain lines snapped tight, gripped by teams of Sand People who were yanked off their feet and dragged along as the thing reared backward in rage.

"*Dank farrik!*" Mando muttered. "It's going back in."

Vanth raised the detonator. "I'm going to hit it."

"No, wait! We only have one shot. We gotta get it out."

The ragtag group of humans and Sand People surged forward, opening fire and bombarding the dragon with projectiles, trying to get it to come after them. It worked all too well. The thing lunged forward again, charging after them, bellowing its fury.

"Now?" Vanth asked.

"Not yet," Mando said. "It's gotta come out further."

The beast tore forward, jaws opening somehow even wider, and belched forth a nauseating glob of acid that splashed onto a group of Tuskens, causing them to dissolve beneath its searing poison.

"Almost . . ." Mando said, "almost . . . now!"

Vanth hit the detonator. The explosion hit the thing's underbelly, sending a tremendous shockwave through the layers of canyon wall and knocking Tuskens and humans alike off their feet. The howl of pain and anger shuddered the world around them like an earthquake.

As the dust cleared, they saw the dragon again—all two hundred meters of it, rising back up with another spray of acid from its mouth.

"It's picking us off like womp rats!" Vanth shouted. "Let's get after it!"

Mando switched on his jet pack, and the marshal followed suit, the two of them swooping toward the thing, firing blasters at it—although at this point the assault only seemed to be making the beast mad.

"This ain't doing a thing," Vanth said in disgust.

"Just keep shooting!" Landing again, Mando looked

over at a nearby bantha loaded down with explosives. "I've got an idea," he said. "You still have that detonator?"

"Take it," Vanth said. "What's the plan?"

"You're gonna take care of the Child," Mando said.

"What are you gonna do?"

"I don't know, but wish me luck."

Before the marshal had time to respond, Mando reached over and hit Vanth's jet pack, causing the marshal to blast away into the sky. Then, stepping toward the bantha, Mando armed the explosive charges strapped to its sides, reining in the creature to prevent it from bolting out of sheer panic.

Then the dragon was upon him. Its enormous jaws clamped down on the bantha and the Mandalorian in a single gulp as the dragon's head vanished beneath the sand.

Not far away, Cobb Vanth fell out of the sky and smashed against the ground with a painful grunt, rolling to a stop in a cloud of sand and dirt. He yanked off his helmet and caught his breath, gazing out at the silence. Off in the distance, he saw the Child that the bounty hunter had asked him to protect, its wrinkled head poking up out of the saddlebag. Even from there, the marshal could tell the kid was worried.

Where was the Mandalorian?

Then the rumbling came again, louder than before. Townspeople and Tuskens raced for cover as the dragon rose up from beneath the ground, jaws wide, and Mando flew out of its mouth using his jet pack.

From below, Vanth saw the bounty hunter still had the detonator in his hand.

He watched as Mando hit the switch.

For a split second the dragon's belly bloated from the force of the internal explosion, and then its entire midsection ruptured in a volcanic spray of fire and tissue, blasting sand and silt in a thousand directions.

Mando landed and turned to look back at what remained of the smoking carcass. All around him, Tuskens and townspeople alike cheered in victory. They'd done it. All of them together.

And somehow they'd managed not to kill each other in the process.

Later, after the Tuskens had begun stripping the meat from the dragon's spine and ribs, the marshal went to find Mando. The bounty hunter had packed and tied a huge chunk of dragon flesh to the front of his speeder bike and was preparing to head out.

"Sorry," Mando said. "I didn't have time to explain."

"No need." Vanth handed over the armor and the helmet. "This was well earned."

"It was my pleasure," Mando said, offering his hand, and the other man shook it.

The marshal smiled. "I hope our paths cross again."

"As do I."

"Oh," Vanth said, "and you tell your people I wasn't the one that broke that." He nodded at the dented armor. Behind them, a celebratory howl rang out, and they both looked over to see a Tusken holding up a giant glistening pearl that he'd recovered from deep in the dragon's gut. Treasure could be found in the most unlikely places in this bleak and desolate land.

Mando mounted the bike, the Child safely at his side, and fired up the engine. It would be a long way back to Mos Eisley, and they needed to get going. As he headed off into the twin sunsets, he was unaware that he was being watched by a figure standing on a cliff overlooking the scene below.

After a moment, the figure pulled a cloak over his bald head and turned to go.

There would be time to find the Mandalorian again. Soon.

CHAPTER 05

THEY DIDN'T GET FAR.

Mando's speeder bike was whizzing along beneath Tatooine's twin suns, heading into a canyon with the armor on one side and the Child on the other, when a hidden rope sprang up from the sand between the rocks. The rope snapped tight, clotheslining the bike and sending the Mandalorian and his baggage airborne. For a moment the world dissolved into a whirling blur. The bike flew end over end, bounced twice, and exploded.

Hitting the ground with a grunt, Mando spun around in time to see two ragged-looking bounty hunters coming out from behind the rocks, already firing in his direction. A third, smaller hunter joined them.

"Get the Child!" one of them snapped.

Blaster in hand, Mando fired at the smaller figure,

hitting him in the leg, as the two other assailants came at him, along with yet another attacker wielding a sword. How many of them were there? Mando took out the saber wielder with a blow to the face, then spun around to confront the other two in a volley of quick punches and thrusts. They were on either side of him then, pinning him against a rock. Glancing up, Mando saw the smaller hunter had returned and was pointing a blaster rifle directly at him. Hardly thinking, Mando fired his cable and yanked the rifle toward him, ducking just as the blaster took out both hunters.

Getting up, he saw the smaller figure standing there, holding the Child, with a knife held close to the kid's chest.

"Wait!" Mando said. "Don't hurt the Child."

The hunter didn't move.

"If you put one mark on him," Mando said, "there's no place you will be able to hide from me." He spoke calmly, in a reasonable tone. "We can strike a bargain. There's a lot of value in this wreckage. Take your pick. But leave the Child."

The hunter glanced nervously at what remained of the speeder bike, then returned his gaze to Mando, pointing his knife at the jet pack and then at the ground between them.

"Okay." Mando reached back, unfastening the jet pack and placing it on the ground. "Here. It's yours. Take it. It's okay."

The hunter edged forward, set the Child down, and scooped up the jet pack, then scurried away. The Child ran to Mando, and he lifted him up.

"You okay?" Mando asked, and the Child gurgled in acknowledgment.

As the hunter hurried off with his newfound treasure, Mando activated the jet pack from the remote switch on his gauntlet. An instant later, the hunter flew up into the air with a startled shriek, pinwheeling through a series of loops. Mando and the Child watched as he plunged out of the sky to land with a faint but audible thud.

Mando piloted the pack down to the ground. It landed in front of them and fell over, and Mando got to work gathering up the debris.

From there on, he'd have to walk.

Beneath the scorching suns, the Mandalorian made his way forward with the Child in a sling and the armor, the jet pack, and other parcels dangling from a piece of the speeder bike, balanced across his shoulders like a yoke. By the time he arrived at the gates of Mos Eisley, it was dark.

He found Peli Motto in a back corner of the cantina, playing sabacc with what looked like a giant ant.

"I don't know," she was saying as Mando approached. "It looks like someone's gonna be going home empty-handed." She glanced up at the bounty hunter, not terribly surprised to see him again, taking note of the helmet and armor. "You finally found a Mandalorian and you killed him?"

"He wasn't a Mandalorian," Mando said. "I bought this armor off of him, though."

"What did that set you back?"

"Killed the krayt dragon for him."

She raised an eyebrow. "Oh, is that all?"

"He was my last lead on finding other Mandalorians."

The ant made a noise, some form of speech that Mando didn't recognize, although Peli seemed to understand him. "Well, you might be in luck," she said. "Dr. Mandible here says he can connect you with someone who can help you, if you cover his call this round. It's what he said."

"What's the bet?" Mando asked.

"Five hundred."

"That's a high-stakes game."

"Hey," she said, "he's on a hot streak."

The ant-like being nodded, and Mando dropped the credits into the pot.

"Is the pot right?" Peli asked, then flipped over her cards. "Ha! Idiot's array! Pay up, thorax!" She collected the cash with a victorious flourish.

"I thought you said he was on a hot streak," Mando said.

She waved a dismissive hand at him. "Ah, stop your crying. You'll rust." Across the table, Dr. Mandible made another clicking sound, and she translated. "He says the contact will rendezvous at the hangar. They'll tell you where to find some Mandalorians. That's what you wanted, right?"

"Yes."

"More importantly, did you bring back any of that dragon meat?" She peered at him suspiciously. "Better not have any maggots on it. I don't like maggots."

Back at the docking bay, the Child watched with eager delight as one of Peli's pit droids roasted the dragon meat Mando had brought back, the steak rotating on the makeshift rotisserie of a turbine engine until it was grilled to perfection. "Hey," Peli said, coming out of her office, "don't overcook it, Treadwell! I like it medium rare! I'm not some Rodian, for crying out loud." Hands on hips, she turned her attention to Mando. "All right, here's the deal. A Mandalorian covert is close. It's in this sector, one system trailing."

"Are they the ones that left Nevarro?" Mando asked.

"Don't know. All I do know is that the contact will lead you to them."

"How much will it cost me?"

"Well, that's the great news," Peli said. "It's free. Aside from a finder's fee, of course."

"What's the not-great news?" Mando asked.

"Nothing," she said. "It's all great."

But it wasn't, and Mando sensed it even before Peli introduced the passenger he'd be taking with him—a shy, amphibious woman carrying a glowing cylinder full of a floating mass of eggs. Peli explained that the woman was spawning, and she needed her eggs fertilized by the equinox or her family line would end. The "skank in the scud pile," as Peli put it, was that Mando would be forced to travel at sublight speed for the entire length of the journey. Jumping to hyperspace would kill the eggs.

"No deal," Mando said. "Moving fast is the only thing that keeps me safe."

"These are mitigating circumstances."

Mando looked at the mother with her jar of eggs. The Child was gazing at them, too.

"Do you want to find the other Mandalorians or not?" Peli asked.

In the end, the question answered itself. Mando had no choice, which was how he found himself and his new passenger side by side in the *Crest*'s cockpit, jetting off from Mos Eisley spaceport. The Frog Lady sat in the jump seat as Mando kept the ship's velocity at a manageable level. "Now I'm going to ask you to stay strapped in whenever you're seated," he said. "Traveling sublight is a bit dicey these days. Whether it's pirates or warlords, someone either ends up with a nice chunk of change or your ship."

The Frog Lady replied in a series of worried croaks, her large black eyes communicating some equally unintelligible message.

"I don't speak whatever language that is," Mando said. "You speak Huttese?" Then, for good measure, he repeated the question in Huttese.

The Frog Lady blinked at him. Translation: No.

The eggs were orange and gooey-looking, floating in their bath of blue fluid. The Child stared at them for a moment, mesmerized, then reached in, pulled one out, and popped it into his mouth.

"No!" the Mandalorian called out, running over and pulling the Child away from the egg jar. "That is not food. Don't do that again."

The Child burped.

"Nap time," Mando said, and he placed the Child in the hammock and sank back into his own berth. What next?

It didn't take long to find out.

The ship's warning signal roused him and sent him scrambling up to the cockpit, where the Frog Lady was fast asleep in the jump seat. Looking out, Mando immediately saw the reason for the alert. A pair of X-wings had pulled up on either side of the *Crest*, and one of the pilots was hailing him over the comm.

"*Razor Crest* Em-One-Eleven," the pilot said. "Come in, *Razor Crest*. Do you copy?"

"This is *Razor Crest*," Mando said. "Is there a problem?"

"We noticed your transponder is not emitting."

"Yes," the Mandalorian said. "I'm pre-Empire surplus. I'm not required to run a beacon."

"That was before," the pilot said. "This sector is under New Republic jurisdiction. All craft are required to run a beacon identifying their ship and crew affiliation."

"Thank you for letting me know. I'll get right on it."

"Not a problem," the pilot said. "Safe travels."

There was silence. Mando waited for the X-wings to depart, but they hung in there on either side of him. Was there something else they were waiting for, some final bit of protocol he'd overlooked? "May the Force be with you," he said haltingly.

"And also with you," the pilot said. Another pause, and then, in that same casual tone: "Just one more thing."

That was when Mando knew he was in trouble. He didn't know the exact nature of the trouble, or how much screaming from the Frog Lady would be involved, but he recognized it was coming. "Yes?"

"I'm going to need you to send us a ping," the pilot said. "We're out here sweeping for Imperial holdouts."

"I'll let you know if I see any," Mando said.

"I'm still going to need you to send us that ping."

"Yeah," Mando said, "I don't seem to have that hardware online."

"We can wait."

Now the Frog Lady was awake and watching him. Mando turned his attention to the instrument array. "Yeah," he said, "it doesn't seem to be, uh, working."

"That's too bad," the pilot said. "If we can't confirm you're not Imperial you're going to have to follow us to the outpost at Adelphi. They'll run your tabs."

"Oh, wait," Mando said. "There it is. Transmitting now." The Frog Lady was croaking, starting to panic. Mando glanced at her. "Be quiet!"

"What was that?" the pilot asked, voice sharpening.

"Uh, nothing. The hypervac is . . . drawing off the exhaust manifold." His passenger was croaking louder, mouth open and eyes bulging with fear. Outside, Mando saw the X-wings deploying their S-foils into attack position, never a good sign. When the pilot spoke again, the casual tone in his voice was gone, replaced by a stern note of authority.

"Was your craft in the proximity of New Republic Correctional Transport *Bothan-Five*?"

Mando paused for a split second to consider his next move, then decided to let the ship answer for him. Gripping the throttle, he sent the *Razor Crest* into a power dive through the cloudy atmosphere of the planet below.

That was when the Frog Lady started screaming.

CHAPTER 06

MANDO NEEDED a diversion. Flying low across a snow-covered mountain pass of Maldo Kreis, he spun the *Razor Crest* around, firing on a glacial arch. The frozen peak exploded, spewing frost and ice fragments across the windscreens of the two X-wings. The distraction allowed Mando to drop out of view, and a moment later the two New Republic ships sailed by as he settled to the ground.

So far, so good—until the *Crest* abruptly lurched. The Frog Lady gasped, and Mando felt the vessel tilting, their cargo clattering and spilling in the hold, as the entire frozen surface gave way beneath them. More screams from his amphibious passenger. They fell—he wasn't sure how far—and landed with a terrible, splintering crash.

All the rest was darkness.

Coming to some uncertain time later, Mando opened his eyes. It was bitter cold inside the cockpit. The ship's canopy was cracked from impact, the glass iced over, and in all likelihood that was only the beginning of what the *Crest* had broken in its fall.

They appeared to be trapped inside some kind of ice cavern. Over in the jump seat, the Frog Lady was blue and shivering. Mando helped her to her feet, heard the frightened crying that didn't require translation.

"I'll find your eggs," he said. "Don't worry. Gotta get you some blankets. Keep you warm." He fired up the heater and descended the ladder to the cargo hold, wading through the spilled debris to assess the damage. The hull was split, with snow drifting in and cables dangling limp, and everything was covered in a layer of frost and ice. Sparks spat and flew from the damaged electrical conduits in the walls. Up above, he could hear the Frog Lady's distraught wails.

"Hang on!" he shouted. "I'm looking for your eggs!" Trudging to the bunk, he opened the hatch and checked the Child's hammock, but the Child wasn't there.

"Where are you?" Mando asked, and the sound of slurping caught his attention. Turning, he pulled back a tarp and found the Child underneath, clutching the cylinder and helping himself to a post-crash snack.

"No!" Mando said. "I told you not to do that!" He picked up the cylinder, counting the eggs, and heard the Frog Lady again in the cockpit. "Found them!" Then, looking at the Child, who was in the process of slurping up another egg, he asked: "How many did you eat?"

The Child burped.

The temperature continued to plummet. Mando sat huddled with the Child and the Frog Lady in the cargo hold. His amphibious passenger was bundled in blankets, and Mando could see how badly the cold was affecting her—her metabolism was not built to tolerate this climate. But self-preservation wasn't her main concern. She continued to check the temperature of the eggs, the digital readout going lower as the day dragged on.

Mando had provided the passenger and the Child with a tin of rations that he'd heated on the hearth, delivering the makeshift meal with a dose of grim news.

"If you haven't guessed," he said, "we're in a tight spot. The main power drive is not responding and the hull has lost its integrity." Rising, he began to collect some of the tools he'd need to begin repairs. "I suspect the temperature will drop significantly when night falls. We'll have a better idea of our prospects at that time."

The Frog Lady replied in a fearful croak. Mando shook his head.

"I'm sorry, lady, I don't speak frog. Whatever it is, it can wait until morning. I recommend you get some sleep." Crossing his arms, he settled back against the bulkhead and closed his eyes.

◆

"Wake up, Mandalorian."

Mando jerked upright and drew his blaster. The mechanized voice was both frightening and familiar—it was the voice of Zero, the malevolent droid he'd contended with during an ill-fated prison break. The one that had tried to kill the Child.

The droid was peering down at him from the wall, its disembodied head brought back to life like something out of a particularly vivid nightmare.

"This cannot wait until morning," Zero said.

That was when Mando saw it—the Frog Lady had wired a microphone into the droid's head and was using it as a translation tool.

"Don't be alarmed," she said with Zero's voice. "I

bypassed the droid's security protocols and accessed its vocabulator."

"What are you doing?" Mando said. "That droid is a killer."

The Frog Lady continued as if she hadn't heard him. "These eggs are the last brood of my life cycle. My husband has risked his life to carve out an existence for us on the only planet that is hospitable to our species. We fought too hard and suffered too much to resign ourselves to the extinction of our family line. I must demand that you hold true to the deal that you agreed to." She paused, and the soft whimper that escaped her throat spoke more emotion than the words themselves.

"Look, lady," Mando said, "the deal is off. We're lucky if we get off this frozen tomb with our lives."

"I thought honoring one's word was a part of the Mandalorian code," the Frog Lady continued. Even Zero's vocabulator couldn't disguise the sadness in her words. "I guess those are just stories for children."

Mando glanced over at the Child, who was looking back at him. Picking up his tools, he sighed and glanced at the Frog Lady.

"This was not part of the deal," he said, and stepped out into the cold.

CHAPTER 07

OUTSIDE THE WIND was howling through the ice cavern. Snow and ice crunched beneath Mando's boots as he inspected the exterior damage to the *Razor Crest*. It was even worse than he'd expected. Much of the outer skin of the ship had been sheared off, exposing inner machinery. Hydraulic fluid stained the snow. Getting airborne again would require nothing short of a miracle.

He stopped and looked up. There was little there except frozen white emptiness, an eerie waste filled with blue shadows, with no visible indication of how they were going to get out.

Squatting, he set to work with the tools.

There was a gibbering noise behind him, and when he glanced over his shoulder, he saw the Child standing there, pointing at the ship.

"How about you come over here and give me a hand," Mando said. "Make yourself useful."

Instead of coming closer, the Child turned and scurried away in the snow, toward the other side of the Crest.

"Hey, kid," Mando said. "Where are you going? Come back here."

Then he stopped, seeing what the Child had been pointing at. In front of him, leading away from the cracked hull, were a series of tracks in the snow. Mando switched on the visual enhancement in his visor and stared at the fading heat signature of the footprints continuing down the long ice tunnel.

"When did she go?" he asked.

The Child answered in a babble of sounds. With little choice, Mando bent down and scooped him up, then began to follow the tracks deeper into the cavern, listening to the muffled crunch of snow beneath his feet.

And then something else—a gurgling liquid sound, accompanied by a sudden spike in the heat signature. Gazing ahead, he saw an open chamber, its walls dripping around him. Long stalactites of ice dangled overhead like glistening teeth.

Warmth was the last thing he'd expected to find in this frozen cave, and yet somehow the Frog Lady had found it. In the center of the chamber, a hot spring exhaled clouds of steam into the frigid air. The empty egg cylinder sat at the edge of the spring, and Mando saw the Frog Lady submerged up to her chin in the warm water, surrounded by her bobbing eggs.

"There you are," Mando said. "You can't leave the ship. It's not safe out here." Setting the Child down, he knelt next to the pool. "Let's gather these up."

The Frog Lady croaked out her protest.

"I know it's warm," he told her, "but night's coming fast, and I can't protect you out here." He began gathering the eggs and putting them into the cylinder, and realized that the Child was also reaching for an egg, no doubt with different intentions. Mando pointed at him.

"No," he said. "No!"

The Child whimpered and sniffed the air, then saw something even more enticing on the far side of the chamber.

There were other eggs down there.

Bigger ones.

Wandering over, the Child began to look at these strange new eggs, sniffing what promised to be an exotic frozen meal. He reached down and peeled an egg open to expose a tiny insectoid creature surrounded by strands and webs of sticky goo. He pulled it out and stuck the entire thing in his mouth, crunching down on its outer shell and tasting the soft meat inside, cooing at the flavor spreading across his palate.

As he chewed, he scarcely noticed the other eggs around him beginning to shiver and crack.

Until it was too late.

Over by the hot spring, Mando heard the Child crying. When he glanced up, he saw the Child scurrying toward him, visibly frightened, and the Mandalorian immediately saw why. The eggs encrusting the floor of the cavern had all begun to hatch, spewing forth dozens—and then hundreds—of chittering ice spiders.

Mando scooped up the Child in one hand and the glass cylinder of eggs in the other. He was aware of the Frog Lady gazing deeper into the cavern, heard the rumbling as it grew louder, and an instant later a large creature appeared with a growling snarl.

The ice spider lunging toward them was enormous. Its gaping mouth was lined with teeth. It was plainly not happy to find them in its lair.

"Go!" Mando shouted, gesturing. "Go! Go! Back to the ship!"

They sprinted forward, with the spiders scurrying

and scampering along behind them, closing in along the curved sides of the ice tunnel. Turning, Mando fired at them, blasting the nearest ones, then kept running. In front of him, the Frog Lady had dropped onto all fours and started to hop, kicking up frantic puffs of snow as she vaulted forward.

Somehow the massive spider was above them then, its legs and swollen thorax thinly visible through the layer of ice. Mando activated a handful of explosive charges and slapped them against the frozen walls. The blast rocked the cavern, sending down layers of rock and ice on all sides. But in the end, it didn't make a difference.

The spiders were coming closer.

Up ahead, he saw the ship.

Mando, the Child, and the Frog Lady squeezed through the broken hull, charging across the cargo bay and up the ladder, the terrible sound of the spiders' legs following close behind. Mando found he could get the hatchway only partially closed—more spiders were piling up on the outside, forcing their way in with terrible eagerness, crawling into the cockpit. He fired at them, reducing whole clusters of the creatures to globs of foulsmelling ooze. He heard the Child shriek behind him, and whirled around to see a spider clutching the baby's head. There was another blast, and the ice spider burst apart. Looking over, Mando saw the Frog Lady holding the blaster that had killed the thing.

Mando switched on the flamethrower on his wrist and sent a jet of flame into the gap where the spiders were trying to get through, burning them to a crisp. They made a hideous, high-pitched squeal as they died, and at last the others began to retreat.

Finally, he got the hatch closed.

Outside, though, the creatures kept coming, swarming the ship in even greater numbers. Their legs made clinking sounds on the frosty glass of the viewport above them. Mando jumped into the seat and fired up the engines.

"Strap yourselves in," he said. "This better work."

Outside the things had accumulated so thickly that they'd begun blocking out the light. The Child was whimpering steadily, eyes wide with terror.

"I got limited visibility," Mando said. "It's gonna be a bumpy ride."

He pulled back the throttle, the thrusters whining with effort, and the Crest began to rise.

Then, suddenly, it all crashed down again.

The giant spider had landed on top of the ship and

slammed it to the floor of the cavern, legs straddling the upper level of the ship, smashing through the dome of the cockpit. Through the viewport Mando could see the thing's proboscis, the horrific suctioning mouth filled with teeth, its black eyes filled with hunger.

Within seconds, the monster outside would rip its way in, and that would be it. Mando could hear the Frog Lady behind him in the jump seat, the soft croaking sounds she made as she saw her worst fears realized. She would never get her eggs fertilized, and they were all going to die in this frozen cave, all because—

Sudden blaster fire erupted outside—a volley of bolts riddling the creature, hammering it until the thing went rigid, trembled, and fell still, then slid off the front of the *Razor Crest*. Its legs curled up around it in a death clench.

Mando looked around, not sure what was happening. He ducked out of the cockpit and down into the cargo hold, hearing the blaster fire continuing outside. The smaller ice spiders were mostly gone, leaving behind crystalline webs that would've been beautiful if they weren't so nightmarish. To his left, a straggling ice spider scrambled up the hull, and before Mando could react, a blaster bolt tore it apart.

Stepping out through the cracked hull, he saw who was shooting.

The X-wings had landed inside the cavern. The two pilots who had hailed him earlier stood in their cockpits with blaster rifles in hand, finishing off the last of the spiders with calm precision. Mando stood motionless, with his own blaster still raised in front of him, taking in the unlikely scene. All the other spiders were dead or had retreated. The floodlights of the New Republic fighters bathed the cavern in a serene and reassuring light.

The pilots stopped firing and looked at him.

"We ran the tabs on the *Razor Crest*," one of the pilots called out. "You have an arrest warrant for the abduction of Prisoner Ex-Six-Nine-Eleven."

Mando didn't say anything.

"However," the pilot continued, "onboard security records show that you apprehended three priority culprits from the Wanted Register."

Slowly, the Mandalorian holstered his blaster.

"Security records also show that you put your own life in harm's way to try to protect that of Lieutenant Davan from the New Republic Correctional Corps," the pilot said. "Is this true?"

"Am I under arrest?" Mando asked.

"Technically, you should be. But these are trying times."

Mando took a step toward them. "What say I forgo the bounties on those three criminals and you two help me fuse my hull back together so I can get off this frozen rock."

"What say you fix that transponder," the pilot replied, "and we don't vaporize that antique the next time we patrol the Rim."

As if to punctuate the finality of the matter, the pilots closed the canopies on their fighters and lifted off in a spray of flame and snow, leaving Mando standing next to his ship with an enormous dead spider draped over it like the world's ugliest hunting trophy. After a moment, he turned and went back into the cargo hold.

The Frog Lady was shivering inside, cradling her cylinder of eggs, the Child bundled up beside her.

"All right," Mando said, "I'm gonna repair the cockpit enough for us to limp to Trask. There's nothing I can do about the main hull's integrity so we're going to have to get cozy in the cockpit. It's the only thing I can pressurize."

He went to work with the welder, finishing repairs on the spider-damaged cockpit. The results were far from perfect, but as he sealed the hatch, he hoped it would be enough. "Okay," he said. "Repairs all done. Let's see if we can get this thing going once and for all."

As the boosters fired, the *Razor Crest* trembled, groaned, and finally snapped loose from the ice. The navicomputer screen pulsed to life as the ship maneuvered through a hole barely bigger than it was, clipping the jagged rim, rising from the frigid depths like a creature reborn. Moments later, they'd cleared the atmosphere of Maldo Kreis and were heading outward through space.

"Wake me up if someone shoots at us," Mando said tiredly, "or if that door gets sucked off its rails."

The Frog Lady and the Child both looked at him.

"I'm kidding. If that happened, we'd all be dead. Sweet dreams."

Settling back, he closed his eyes. In the jump seat, the Frog Lady saw the Child eyeing the cylinder of eggs, and she protectively clutched it closer. The Child uttered a soft coo, reassuring her that his intentions were good, and when she finally looked away, he quietly slipped one last stolen egg into his mouth and swallowed.

CHAPTER 08

THE *RAZOR CREST* was plummeting out of the sky.

Mando and his two passengers had been fast asleep when they'd passed beneath the shadow of Trask, the moon beyond the gas giant Kol Iben. The proximity alert had jolted Mando awake, and he'd immediately realized they were in trouble. The ship's landing array wasn't responding. Without that guidance system, he'd have to attempt a manual reentry, a dicey move under the best of circumstances.

"Once we're through the atmosphere," he said, "there should be just enough fuel to slow us down." Then, as the blue moon loomed through the viewport, approaching fast, he added, "If we don't burn to a crisp first."

On the display screen, alarms were flashing. The ship's heat shields were in the red, the fuel bar dangerously low as the viewport began to turn an unstable, fiery orange with the heat of reentry. Through the glass, Mando could see their destination, a port city nestled on the coastline, coming up way too fast, but there was nothing he could do about it. The Frog Lady hovered beside him, clutching her jar of eggs.

"Come up here," he said. "I need your hands!"

As she crept forward, Mando pointed at the controls.

"That lever needs to stay back," he said. "Can you do that?"

She took hold of the lever and clutched it for dear life as the ship continued to fall. Mando heard the voice of flight control crackling through the comm speaker. "*Razor Crest*, this is Trask flight control. Please reduce your speed to port protocol."

"I'm trying my best here," Mando said. Then, to his newly appointed copilot: "Engage reverse thrusters. Brace!" Slamming the repulsors down, he ignited the ship's retrorockets with the full power of whatever fuel remained in the tank. The entire vessel shuddered with a tortured howl of the repulsors, but they somehow managed to slow the *Crest*'s descent as it closed in on the approaching pier.

"Here we go," Mando said, eyes fixed on the landing pad coming up beneath them. "Nice and easy . . ."

Suddenly and without warning, the fuel gauge dropped to empty. One of the ship's sideways repulsors let out a final, half-hearted toot, and the *Crest* drifted horizontally, missing the pad and splashing down in the water.

Another perfect landing.

◈

The spaceport was a thriving mixture of water vessels and spacecraft, with cargo being transported to and fro. Enormous nets of freshly caught aquatic life swung from cranes, ready to be distributed across that corner of the galaxy. Amid all this, the salvaged *Razor Crest* lay on the dock dripping seawater like the catch of the day.

"Can you fix it?" the Mandalorian asked.

"Fix it?" The Mon Calamari dockworker looked at the battered ship. "No, but I can make it fly."

Mando handed him some credits. "Do what you can."

"I'll fuel it up, if it still holds fuel."

Mando started walking, with the Child's pram hovering at his side, then glanced across the port where a frog man was standing with a seabag over his shoulder. Mando watched as the Frog Lady approached her mate and they ran to each other, croaking with joy. The couple spent a moment gazing with affection at the tank of eggs, their shared love gleaming in their eyes.

The Child was also eyeing the eggs, with a small whimper.

"I know you're hungry," Mando said. "We'll get you something to eat." He turned to the Frog Man, who was croaking his heartfelt appreciation for the safe arrival of his mate and their eggs. "You're welcome. I was told you could lead me to others of my kind?"

The Frog Man croaked and pointed toward the far end of the wharf.

"The inn?" Mando asked. "Over there?"

The Frog Man nodded.

"Thank you," the Mandalorian said. They shook hands, and Mando made his way inside the inn to find whatever awaited him there.

"Have a seat over there," the Mon Calamari server told him as Mando eased his way into the darkened establishment. He took a spot at the barrel-shaped central table. The place was full of hungry diners, not only Mon Calamari but also Quarren, their heavy-browed faces adorned with long tentacles that drooped down over their mouths. "What can I get you?"

"Nothing for me," Mando said, and nodded at the pram floating next to him, where the Child was already gazing expectantly at the server. "A bowl of chowder for my friend."

"These seats are scarce, buddy. Everyone seated needs to eat."

"I can buy something else." The Mandalorian pushed some Calamari flan across the table, offering the proprietor a generous amount of the local currency. "Information. Have you seen others that look like me?"

The server put a bowl in front of the Child and yanked a lever to extend a fat hose from the ceiling, dispensing a chunky portion of chowder into the bowl. "Others with beskar have been through here."

"Who can take me to them?" Mando asked.

"I know someone who might help." Without another word, the server went across the room to talk to a Quarren sailor at another table. Meanwhile the Child had already begun sipping his chowder. Something bubbled inside the bowl, and an instant later a squid-like creature jumped out and attached itself to the Child's face, making him squeak and squeal. Mando jabbed it with his knife, and the thing fell back into the chowder bowl with a plop.

"Don't play with your food," he said.

The server had returned with the Quarren, who sat down beside Mando. "You seek others of your kind."

"Have you seen them?" the Mandalorian asked.

"Aye. I can bring you to them."

"Where?"

"Only a few hours' sail," the Quarren said darkly. "It'll cost you, though."

The sailor wasn't lying. By the time it was all over, the price would be steep indeed.

CHAPTER 09

SOME TIME LATER they were aboard a ramshackle fishing boat headed out to sea, the vessel bouncing and heaving over the waves. Mando was standing on deck, with the Child in his pram beside him, gazing out at the gray expanse of water, when a Quarren approached with a fishing gaff over one shoulder.

"Ever see a mamacore eat?" he inquired. "Quite a sight. Child might take an interest." He gestured toward an open hatchway in the hull of the boat, revealing a large grate and a fishhold full of seawater. "Come on over here, get a good view. Let the kid see."

"All right," Mando said as the Child peered down. "That's close enough."

"There we go," the sailor said as the cage opened, allowing for a net of chum to be dumped inside. The

Child leaned over the edge of the pram for a closer look as bubbles rose to the surface. "She must be hungry. Oftentimes we'll feed her in the early morning, but we missed that because we were going out of port—"

Without warning, the sailor swung the gaff and knocked the Child's pram forward, over the hold. From below, a gigantic sea beast burst up from the surface and swallowed the pram and the Child in one gulp.

"No!" Mando said, and dove into the hold. The Quarren slammed the cage shut, trapping the Mandalorian inside.

"Drown him!" the Quarren shouted. "The beskar is ours!" He and the others jumped down to the top of the cage, thrusting gaffs and sharpened pikes between the bars, jabbing and slashing at Mando's hands, forcing him back down below the surface. The bounty hunter coughed, gasping for air as the blades slashed down at him again. "We're rich, brother! Finish him!"

Mando felt his fingers slipping away from the bars as the weight of his armor dragged him below the surface. Then as the water closed over him, a rain of blaster fire began pouring down from above. Through the steel grate, he saw three Mandalorians with jet packs descending onto the deck. They attacked the Quarren, and although the sailors were experienced fighters, it didn't take long for the Mandalorians to finish them off, knocking one of them overboard and dispensing with the others with a series of hand-to-hand blows that cleared the deck in a matter of seconds.

One of the Mandalorians bent down and lifted the gate to free Mando. "Take my hand."

"There's a creature," Mando said. "It has the Child."

"On it," the second Mandalorian said, and dove in while the first helped Mando across the deck and into a seated position atop a pile of heavy rope.

"The Child," Mando managed. "Help the Child. . . ."

"Don't worry, brother. We've got this."

The cage below them flashed with a series of submerged explosions. Seconds later, the surface buckled and bubbled, and the Mandalorian who'd jumped in flew back out with the silver pram in her hands, landing on the deck.

"Here you go, little one." She pulled the half-crushed lid loose to reveal the Child inside and handed him to Mando.

The bounty hunter looked down at the Child's face with a sigh of relief. Somehow the baby had come through all of that unscathed.

"Thank you," he said to the Mandalorians. "I've been searching for more of our kind."

The Mandalorian in front of him nodded. "Well, lucky we found you first."

"I've been quested to deliver this child," Mando said. "I was hoping that—"

His voice broke off. All three of them were removing their helmets. Mando rose to his feet, taken aback by the ease with which they'd exposed their faces. Two of the Mandalorians were women—the one in the middle, seemingly the leader, had green eyes and red hair held back with a headband. The two that flanked her, a younger woman and a dark-haired man, both regarded Mando with steady gazes.

"Where did you get that armor?" Mando asked.

The woman directly in front of him spoke calmly. "This armor has been in my family for three generations."

"You do not cover your face," Mando said. "You are not Mandalorian."

"He's one of *them*," said the man.

"*Dank farrik*," the other woman cursed softly under her breath.

Mando's voice tightened. "One of what?"

"I am Bo-Katan of Clan Kryze," the red-haired woman said, with the same air of composure. "I was born on Mandalore and fought in the Purge. I am the last of my line." She nodded at the other two standing on either side of her. "This is Koska Reeves and Axe Woves. And you are a Child of the Watch."

"The Watch?" Mando asked, not comprehending.

"Children of the Watch are a cult of religious zealots that broke away from Mandalorian society. Their goal was to reestablish the ancient way."

"There is only one way," Mando said. "The Way of the Mandalore." Without waiting for their response, he turned and ignited his jet pack, blasting off the deck with the Child in one arm.

It was dark when Mando returned to the docks, hoping that the Mon Calamari deckhand had managed at least to refuel the *Razor Crest* in his absence. He wasn't sure where they would go from there, but this place held no more answers for him.

In his arms, the Child squirmed restlessly as they made their way among the piles of crates, ropes, and nets, as if sensing the uncertain future that lay before them.

"Hey, you," someone said, and a Quarren thug stepped into view in front of Mando, a sneer on his face. "You killed my brother."

Mando stopped as more Quarren emerged from the

shadows, a group of intimidating figures, all brandishing weapons.

"Let me pass," he said.

The Quarren chuckled. "I don't think you understand. You killed my brother"—he drew a blaster, aiming it at Mando and the Child—"and now I'm gonna kill your pet."

The Child whimpered. Mando was outnumbered, and fighting his way out might put the Child in danger. He was still trying to decide on his next move when he heard a whoosh of jets as the three Mandalorians he'd encountered earlier soared down from above, landing in front of the Quarren.

"He didn't kill your brother," one of them said. "I did."

The thugs barely had a moment to protest. After a sudden storm of blaster fire, the entire group of Quarren lay dead on the ground.

Mando stared at the trio as they reholstered their weapons.

"Can we at least buy you a drink?" Bo-Katan asked.

◆

Later Mando sat with the three at a corner table in the darkened inn, where they spoke in hushed voices.

"Trask is a black market port," Bo-Katan said. "They're staging weapons that have been bought and sold with plunders of our planet. We're seizing those weapons and using them to retake our homeworld. Once we've done that, we'll seat a new Mandalorian on the throne."

"That planet is cursed," Mando said. "Anyone who goes there dies. Once the Empire knew they couldn't control it, they made sure no one else could, either."

Bo-Katan shook her head. "Don't believe everything you hear. Our enemies want to separate us, but Mandalorians are stronger together."

"That's not part of my plan," Mando said. "I have been quested with returning this child to the Jedi."

Jedi. That word, once spoken, seemed to cast a long shadow over the conversation, a foreboding that hadn't been there before.

"What do you know of the Jedi?" Bo-Katan asked.

"Nothing," Mando said. "I was hoping you would help me by creed."

"I can lead you to one of their kind," she told him, "but first we need your help on our mission."

CHAPTER 10

NIGHT WAS FALLING as they sat on top of the *Razor Crest*, watching the active port. Off in the distance, a large Imperial cruiser sat on the pier, its hull cutting an imposing shape across the pink-and-blue marbled sky as the last glow of daylight drained into the horizon.

"You see that Imperial Gozanti freighter?" Bo-Katan asked. "It's being loaded with weapons as we speak. According to the port's manifest, it's scheduled to depart at first light."

"So we stow away?" Mando asked.

"We've been hitting them pretty hard," Koska said over her shoulder. She was sprawled across the roof of the *Crest* with the casual demeanor of a warrior at rest. "They scan for life-forms as a precaution before pushing back."

"If you want to do this with four," Mando said, "you're going to need the element of surprise."

Bo-Katan nodded. "Exactly. The freighter will maintain trawling speed while inside the shipping lanes and then ascend into orbit. We'll jet up when they're cruising at low speed in atmosphere."

"Troopers?"

"A squad at most," Bo-Katan said.

Axe Woves shook his head. "And they couldn't hit the side of a bantha."

Mando was still unconvinced, but it didn't matter. They'd made up their minds, and he would fight alongside them for better or worse.

They hit the freighter at dawn. Taking out the first half dozen stormtroopers was even easier than Mando had expected. Bo-Katan, Koska, and Axe dispatched the unprepared Imperials so efficiently that for a moment Mando didn't even realize that one of the troopers had managed to trigger the alarm.

The ship's doors sealed and went into lockdown— not that it mattered. Axe knelt and hot-wired the panel, and in seconds they were inside.

Heading down the corridor, Mando saw more troopers responding to the alert. He and the other Mandalorians moved without hesitation, taking them out with blasters and blades, and advancing toward their objective. Seconds later, another wave of soldiers arrived, blasting wildly down the hallway. Bo-Katan nodded at her fellow warriors in silent communication, and they stepped out, firing back with precision and clearing the space in front of them in a matter of minutes.

Stepping over the bodies, Mando followed the other three to the cargo bay.

The freighter's cargo area was a cavernous space loaded with cases of black market Imperial weaponry packed for transport. Ever since the alarm had gone off, the deck officer in charge had been on the comm trying to ascertain the status of the ship's security breach, but there wasn't much information coming.

"What's happening?" he demanded.

An instant later, the security officer replied: "The intruders are heading your way."

"Just hold them off long enough until we can make the jump to hyperspace and rendezvous with the fleet," the captain snapped.

"Copy," the deck officer said nervously. Looking at the troopers, he struggled to summon an air of authority, then turned to the hatchway in front of him, pointing his blaster at the doors. "We need to hold them off until we can make the jump to hyperspace."

The troopers stood at the ready, brandishing the scoped long-blasters they'd taken from one of the cargo containers. Nobody moved. In front of them, the elevator display indicated the pirates' approach—one light going on, then the second, then the third.

The door opened.

The deck officer started shooting.

It didn't matter. The Mandalorians swept forward in a blur, firing at the troopers, wiping them out without hesitation. Hardly thinking, the deck officer turned to one of the troopers. "Close the doors!" he ordered.

"Which ones?"

"All of them! *Close all the doors!*"

The trooper hit the button, and the doors closed behind the Mandalorians. He hit another, and the heavy bay doors closed between the attackers and the troopers, trapping the Mandalorians in the cargo control chamber. The blaster fire stopped abruptly. The deck officer let out a shaky breath and switched on the comm.

"I think we have them trapped, sir."

The captain's voice came back. "Trapped them where?"

"In the cargo control area."

There was a long pause. "Where?"

"In the cargo control ar—"

The enormous bay doors swung open, filling the entire space with the roar of wind. The deck officer let out a horrified shriek as he and the troopers around him were sucked out. Some of them found handholds, clutching the walls, but one by one they lost their grip and let go, skidding down the tilted floor to be plucked out of the hold and hurled into the void.

Bo-Katan shut the bay doors and eased her way out of the cargo control area, into the main hold. She and the others approached the crates of weapons. There was a comlink on the floor, and she could hear the voice of the security officer.

"Come in," the officer was asking. "Do you copy?"

Bo bent down and picked up the comlink. "I copy."

There was silence on the other end. Now that the battle was over, she and the other two Mandalorians had removed their helmets. Mando could see the expressions of supreme self-confidence on their faces.

"Thanks for packing up all this gear so nicely," Bo-Katan said into the microphone. "Imagine what a division of us can do when we get our hands on what's inside all these shiny little boxes."

The captain's voice was tight with barely controlled fury. "If you think you're going to escape with those weapons, you are sadly mistaken. Even if you manage to jettison a few of those crates, we will comb the entire area until you are hunted down and killed."

"Oh, we're not jettisoning anything," Bo-Katan said. "We're taking the entire ship."

Mando looked at her. "What?"

"Put some tea on," she told the captain. "We'll be up in a minute."

Mando was still staring at her. "This is more than I signed up for," he said.

"There is something I need if I am to rule Mandalore," Bo-Katan said. "Something that was once mine. They know where it is and soon, so will I." Her voice was stern, leaving no room for argument. "Regardless, we are taking the ship for the battles ahead."

Hearing all this, Mando thought of the Child. Before they'd launched their attack on the freighter, he'd left the kid with the Frog Lady and her mate, telling them that he would be back soon. Now he wondered when he would see the Child again.

"I got you your weapons," he told Bo-Katan. "I have to return to *my* ship with the foundling."

Bo-Katan was unmoved. "If you want my help

finding the Jedi," she said, "you will help me take this ship."

"You're changing the terms of the deal."

Her eyes glinted as she repeated his own mantra back to him with thinly veiled sarcasm. "This is the Way." Without waiting for his response, she and the others put their helmets back on and started out the door, leaving Mando standing there.

After a moment, he followed.

◆

On the ship's bridge, the captain, security officer, and other crew members stood before a hologram of Moff Gideon above the control panel. The Moff's face was expressionless as he awaited the news.

"What is it, Captain?" Gideon asked.

"Another pirate hijacking," the captain replied.

"Were you able to eliminate them?"

"No," the captain said, struggling to keep his voice steady. At this stage, there was no point in making excuses. "We need backup immediately."

"Are these the same 'pirates' that attacked our other vessels?" Gideon asked.

"They appear to be," the captain said with a gulp, and added, "sir."

"How far have they gotten?"

"They've breached the cargo hold and taken everything but the bridge. We require immediate backup."

Moff Gideon considered the situation for the briefest of moments. "If they've taken that much of the ship," he said, "I'm afraid that's no longer an option." Locking eyes with the captain, he said: "You know what to do."

The hologram flicked off. The security officer turned to the crew member sitting next to him, the two men exchanging glances as the captain brought out his blaster and shot both of them. Their bodies slumped forward.

"Long live the Empire," the captain said.

The Mandalorians were making their way through the deserted hallways when the freighter began to shudder and angled suddenly downward, engines howling from the power dive. Mando understood at once what was happening and heard Bo-Katan shouting back at them in confirmation.

"They're taking the ship down," she said. "Let's move!"

They began charging forward toward the bridge. Rounding the corner, Mando saw guards outside the door spinning around to fire at them, pinning the Mandalorians back.

"How many troopers?" Bo-Katan asked.

Axe Woves peered out. "Six to ten. Two with heavy repeating blasters."

The ship continued to plummet, making it harder to maintain balance, let alone aim at their enemies with any accuracy. Mando and the others clung to handholds to keep from slipping forward. Koska checked the display. "We're losing altitude fast."

"We need to move now," Bo-Katan said.

Blaster fire spewed everywhere around them, bouncing off the walls. "They have too much firepower!" Axe shouted. "There's nowhere to go!"

"Still dropping," Koska said. "Ten thousand."

"We'll never make it to the bridge on time," Axe said.

"Nine thousand," Koska said. "Eight thousand. Seven . . ."

Mando stepped forward, taking out the two remaining explosive charges and activating them. "Cover me," he said.

He stepped into view. An immediate hail of blaster fire slammed into his beskar, hammering the armor and knocking him backward, but he forced himself to keep going, an armed bomb in each hand, toward the bridge door. The troopers kept firing, even as he tossed the explosives down in front of them. An instant later, the area in front of the bridge door was consumed in a plume of flame. As the smoke cleared, the other Mandalorians rushed to join him and they moved onto the bridge.

The captain sat with his back to them, gripping the controls, focused intently on his mission. Bo-Katan and the others yanked him from his seat, and Mando and Koska took the controls, pulling the ship out of its dive.

It wasn't going to work. The freighter was too big, moving too fast. The entire vessel was shaking violently, every bolt straining against the torque that Mando was subjecting it to. He could see the ocean racing toward them, its wrinkled surface sprawling out into gray eternity, ready to consume them.

He gripped the controls, pulling up harder.

Then, finally, at the last possible second, he felt the ship leveling out. It passed right over a fishing vessel and banked upward toward the sky. All the breath left his lungs in a wash of relief, and behind him, he saw that Bo-Katan had shoved the captain against the wall with her gauntlet blade pointed at his face.

"Where is it?" she snapped.

The captain glared at her, face ashen. "Where's what?"

"The Darksaber. Does he have it?"

"If you're asking," the captain said, "you already know."

"I'll let you live," she said, "but you will take me to him."

The captain's expression didn't change. "You might let me live, but he won't."

"No!" But it was too late. Without hesitation, the captain clenched his jaw, biting down on the electrical charge implanted in a back tooth. The high-voltage shock pulsed over his face as his eyes rolled upward, and he fell to the floor.

Bo-Katan lowered her blade and whirled around, furious, but Koska was already thinking ahead. "We have to go," she said. "He sent a distress signal."

"Clear the atmosphere and prepare to jump," Bo-Katan said, and glanced at Mando. "Are you sure you won't join us?"

"There's something I need to do," Mando said.

"The offer stands if you change your mind."

He looked at her intently. "Where can I find the Jedi?"

"Take the foundling to the city of Calodan on the forest planet of Corvus," she said. "There you will find Ahsoka Tano. Tell her you were sent by Bo-Katan." Her voice softened. "And thank you. Your bravery will not be forgotten." This time, when she spoke the words of the creed, it was with genuine sincerity and warmth. "This is the Way."

"This is the Way," Mando said, and turned to leave.

By the time he returned to pick up the Child, the eggs had hatched.

Mando found him with the mother and father frog, gathered around a bowl where a two-legged tadpole was crawling up from the surface. The Child was fascinated by the newborn.

"Thank you for watching him," Mando told the frogs, then he turned to the Child and scooped him up. "Okay, kid. Come on. Let's go." As the baby fussed and struggled in his arms, Mando glanced at the parents. "Congratulations," he said. Walking out with the Child, still protesting, under one arm, Mando shook his head. "No, I have enough pets."

Back at the docks, the Mandalorian gazed at the supposedly repaired *Razor Crest*. The ship was a sloppy mess, patched together with a mixture of welded metal, ropes, and hose clamps. He looked at the Mon Calamari dockworker. "I gave you a thousand credits," he said. "This was the best you could do?"

The dockworker shrugged and handed Mando the receipt. He approved it and took the Child on board.

Inside, nets and ropes dangled from the walls, where they had been used for various types of makeshift repairs. With a sigh, Mando took hold of the controls and activated the main thrusters, feeling them tremble as the ship rose.

"Mon Calamari," he muttered. "Unbelievable."

To complete the experience, a sea creature scampered out from behind a loose sheet of paneling—some kind of multi-limbed parasite with suction cups on its legs, clinging to the wall, making its way eagerly toward the Child. At the last second, Mando reached back and grabbed the thing, tossing it aside. The Child giggled with delight. "I finally know where I'm taking you," Mando said, "but it's gonna be a bumpy ride." He hit a button and the ship lurched violently, leaving the moon behind them as they prepared to jump to hyperspace. "A bumpy ride" might've been an understatement, but they had a long trip ahead of them.

Not much later, the *Razor Crest* was sputtering through space, engines stalling as the cut-rate Mon

Calamari repair job began to disintegrate around them in real time. Down in the cargo hold, the Mandalorian peered down a dark shaft through an open wall, where part of the paneling had been removed. Inside it, on the far end of the access tube, the Child was poised over a partially dismantled circuit board of exposed wiring.

"All right," Mando said, "let's try this again. Do you have the wire?"

The Child, visibly confused, glanced at the wires in both hands, his brow wrinkled.

"Now," Mando said, "you're going to plug the red wire where the blue wire goes on the board. Put the red wire where the blue wire goes, but don't let them touch."

The Child stared at him, still hesitating.

"You see where you took the blue wire off?" Mando asked patiently. "Yes. Now put the red one—no, don't put the blue one back. Put the red one where the blue one was, and the blue one where the red one was. But be careful. They're oppositely charged, so keep them away from each other. Make sure you hold them apart—no, hold them apart—"

Too late. The Child brought the wires together. There was an audible pop of electrical current, and a puff of smoke floated from the scorched hairs on top of the Child's head.

"Are you okay?"

The Child looked at him and blinked.

"Well," Mando said, "it was worth a shot."

Later, as they sat side by side sipping from bowls of stew, the Mandalorian reflected on the situation. "There's no way we're making it to Corvus in this shape. You know, I think we need to visit some friends for repairs. How'd you like to go back to Nevarro?"

The Child cooed and smiled.

CHAPTER 11

THE THIEVES HAD no idea what the original purpose of the antechamber had been, nor did they particularly care. All the broken furniture and fixtures that had once been the workshop of the Mandalorian Armorer were just another hiding place for the sacks of New Republic credits they'd stolen.

These particular robbers were Aqualish, tusked humanoid creatures with fur and large black eyes. All around them, piles of stolen booty rose up in a miniature cityscape of treasure. At the moment, however, they had more pressing things to squabble over, like the fate of the lava meerkat one of them had pulled by the neck from its cage and shoved down onto the chopping block, preparing to hack the poor creature's head off for the cooking pot.

"Hello, little friend," one of the thieves said, raising a nasty-looking cleaver as the meerkat whimpered what was almost certainly going to be its last breath. The round black eyes of the Aqualish seemed to bulge with anticipation. "Won't you be delicious." He was about to swing the blade down when a noise from the far end of the tunnel made them all freeze and look up.

"Someone's here," another of the thieves said. "Go see what that was."

Everyone pointed their blasters at the doorway, and the Aqualish in front stepped forward cautiously, listening—when a sudden blur of motion slammed into him from the shadows, knocking him off-kilter and into the wall.

Cara Dune had arrived.

Marshal Cara Dune.

The thieves started firing at her, but Cara had been anticipating that and was already moving. Using the first Aqualish as a shield, she charged into the ante-chamber, dispensing body blows as she went. She flung a blade at the criminal on the other side of the room, pinning him to the wall, then grabbed the bald head of the Aqualish nearest to her and slammed his face into the table before dispensing with the other using a broken spotchka bottle. When another Aqualish leapt up behind her, Cara slammed him in the face with her elbow, not even bothering to glance back. As the last of the thieves made a desperate lunge for her, she pulled her blaster and dropped him to the floor.

Within moments, the smoke had cleared and the fight was over. Picking up one of the sacks, Cara began to fill it with the stolen loot that would need to be returned to its rightful owners, and heard a soft chirping behind her.

The meerkat crept up onto her shoulder, chattering what she supposed was gratitude to its newfound savior. "Hey," Cara said. "Okay, okay, little guy. No one's eating you today." The creature nuzzled her even as she plucked it from her shoulder and set it on the table. "Go on. You're free. Git."

The creature got up on its hind legs, head raised, and gazed at her lovingly. "Okay," she said. "Look, here you go." She opened a small pouch of food. "That's all I got."

The creature started eating, and she slung the sack of credits over her shoulder and headed out the door.

◆

Mando saw the amused reactions he was getting from his old friends Cara and Greef Carga as they approached his ramshackle ship. The bounty hunter stepped to the end of the gangway and stopped—the ramp wouldn't even go all the way down.

"Looks like someone could use some repairs," Greef said.

Mando jumped the rest of the way and walked over to the magistrate, taking the man's hand in greeting. "How's my credit around here?"

"I think something can be arranged." Greef looked over at Cara. "Isn't that right, Marshal?"

Cara smiled at the Child in Mando's arms. "I'm sure we can work something out."

"I'll get my best people on it." Greef gestured to the workers in the loading area. "Hey, fellas. Let's fix this man's ship. I want it as good as new." Then with a broad smile, he turned his attention to the Child, lifting him from Mando's arms. "And you, come here, little one! Has Mando been taking good care of you? Have you been taking good care of *him*?"

Still grinning, Greef carried the Child away, leaving Mando and Cara to follow him toward town. As they walked through the streets of Nevarro, the Mandalorian couldn't believe how much things had changed. The shops and bodegas were open, freshly painted and refurbished, and families strolled around without fear of the criminal element he remembered being pervasive the last time he was there. The city seemed to be flourishing.

"Looks like you two have been busy," Mando said.

"I myself have been steeped in clerical work," Greef said ruefully. "Marshal Dune here is to be thanked for cleaning up the town."

As they walked through the town square, Mando glanced up at a statue of IG-11, erected in honor of the droid's heroic sacrifice. They stopped in front of the public house where he and the others had faced off against Moff Gideon on his previous trip. "I'm surprised this place is still standing."

Cara smiled. "Wait till you see inside."

Stepping through the doorway, Mando couldn't believe his eyes. The bar had been transformed into a school. Children sat in rows of desks, looking up at the protocol droid who stood in front of them pointing out floating models of planets on a large display tablet.

"Things have changed a lot around here," Cara said.

Greef carried the Child toward an empty desk. "We're going to leave the little one here so we can talk business."

"Wait." Mando stepped forward. "Wherever I go, he goes."

"Mando, please," the magistrate said. "Where we're going, you don't want to take a child. Trust me."

Greef settled the Child into the seat on the far side of the classroom, and the three of them made their way out. The other children all turned in their desks to stare at the new arrival, whispering and leaning in for a closer look. The Child, meanwhile, was gazing with real interest at the student sitting next to him, who had a small parcel of blue cookies. He held out his hand hopefully, but the boy shook his head.

"No!" he whispered, and returned his attention to the teacher. After a moment, the Child held his arm out again, focused more intently than ever on the cookies.

When the boy glanced down, the entire package of sweets was gone. He turned to look at the Child, who was happily munching away, his lips already stained blue.

The Mythrol sitting in Greef Carga's office recognized Mando right away and let out a cloud of panic through his pores.

"I believe you two have met," the magistrate said drily.

"I'm surprised to see you here," Mando said to his former bounty.

The Mythrol gulped. "Right back at ya."

"Mythrol here's taken care of my books since he was a pollywog," said Greef, "but then he disappeared one day after a bit of 'creative accounting.' Isn't that right?"

"Magistrate Karga was generous enough to let me work off my debt," the Mythrol said, eyes flicking to Greef with a desperate smile. "Thank you, by the way."

"Three hundred and fifty years," Greef said, "but who's counting?"

Cara stepped in, ready to be finished with the pleasantries. "Can we talk business?"

"I'm only here for repairs," Mando told her.

"Which will take a while," Greef said. "Which means you'll have free time on your hands, right? And we could really use your help."

"Help how?" Mando asked.

The magistrate pushed a button, activating a line-vector display in front of them, a holographic map of the planet.

"This is Nevarro," Cara said, and pointed. "We're here. This entire area is the green zone. But over here"—she indicated a distant region of the map—"is the problem."

Before Mando could ask, Greef Karga was already answering the question for him. "It's an old Imperial base."

The Mandalorian has been quested to reunite the Child with his own kind.

While searching for other Mandalorians on Tatooine, Mando encounters Marshal Cobb Vanth, who wears Mandalorian armor found in the desert.

The *Razor Crest* is pursued by pilots from the New Republic.

Mando and the Child take refuge on a snow-covered planet that hides deadly creatures.

Mando and the Child are rescued from pirates by Bo-Katan of Mandalore.

Mando helps the other Mandalorians take over an Imperial remnant ship in return for information about the Jedi.

Greef Karga is happy to see the Child again.

The Child is left at a local school for safekeeping. Will he manage not to cause any trouble?

Bo-Katan tells the Mandalorian to seek out Ahsoka Tano, a former Jedi.

Ahsoka tells Mando she cannot train the Child—whose name is Grogu—because he is too attached to Mando.

Grogu reaches out through the Force from the seeing stone on Tython.

Boba Fett arrives on Tython—along with Fennec Shand—in search of his stolen armor.

Moff Gideon's dark troopers are sent to capture Grogu!

Boba Fett agrees to help Mando rescue Grogu in return for his armor.

Moff Gideon holds the Darksaber as he prepares to stop the Mandalorian from taking Grogu.

The Mandalorian uses a staff of beskar against the Darksaber!

Mando offers the Darksaber to Bo-Katan, but she cannot accept it as it must be earned in battle.

A strange cloaked visitor arrives on Moff Gideon's ship—the Jedi Luke Skywalker!

Mando shows his face to Grogu as they say goodbye.

Luke Skywalker takes Grogu to continue his Jedi training.

He described the rest of it simply enough, using the schematic to illustrate. The heavily fortified base was perched at the top of a lava canyon. Mando could see the turrets above and the massive bay door that opened into the canyon.

"It's where all those troops came from when we defeated Moff Gideon," Cara said. "This base has been here since the Imperial expansion. It's got a skeleton crew, but for some reason it hasn't been abandoned."

"There's a lot of heavy weaponry in that place that the black market would love to dismantle and get their hands on," Greef added.

"And you want to mop up the last of the Imperial force before they do," Mando said.

"Mando," the magistrate said, "I just want them off my planet."

The Mandalorian was still studying the hologram, the base and its fortifications, imagining the challenges and risks of what they were proposing. It would be dangerous; there was no way around that. At this point, however, he supposed that his participation in the mission was no longer in doubt.

"All right," he said. "I'm in."

CHAPTER 12

THE LANDSCAPE was barren, seemingly empty of all life, as they threaded their way through the canyon lands. The Mythrol was behind the controls of the speeder, looking utterly miserable about being dragged along on the trip. Cara was riding shotgun, with Mando and Greef Karga in the back.

"The whole place is powered by a reactor." Cara raised her voice to be heard over the rush of wind. "We sneak in, overload the reactor, and get out of there."

"Let's be fast," Mando said. "And keep the speeder running."

As they approached the facility looming high above the canyon floor, the Mythrol appeared even more troubled. "How close do you want me to drop you off?"

"How about the front door?" Greef said.

"That's a little close for a civilian, don't you think?"

"I got two choices for you," Greef said. "You take us in and I knock a hundred years off your debt . . ."

"Or?"

"Or I leave you here in the lava flats to walk home with whatever's left in your humidity vest," the magistrate said.

The Mythrol let out a gloomy sigh. "That's not much of a choice, is it?" He drove them closer, finally approaching the hardened security hatch, and brought the speeder to a halt as Mando and the others leapt out. The door was a flat square plate of imposing-looking metal tucked deep beneath the looming shadow of the base's launchpad, a hundred meters overhead. Mando went to work on the security access panel, but it was no use.

"Controls are useless," he said. "They're melted."

"Probably not rated for lava," Greef said.

Cara shook her head in disgust. "Imperial trash."

Mando glanced up at the overhanging launchpad. "Hold tight," he said. Activating his jet pack, he blasted straight up the canyon wall, leaving the others standing there. A moment later they heard a scream, and the body of a stormtrooper crashed to the ground in front of them. Then the elevator opened. Greef and Cara stepped inside, and the magistrate looked back at the Mythrol.

"Are you coming in or what?"

"I'll take my chances down here," the Mythrol said, "but thank you."

Cara glanced down the canyon. "Well, when the lava tide comes in, give us a holler. We'll drop you a rope."

The Mythrol blinked, reconsidered, and followed them inside.

When the elevator doors opened on the top floor of the base, the first thing Greef, Cara, and the Mythrol saw were the bodies of stormtroopers strewn about. Mando stood waiting for them.

"Empty base, huh?" he asked.

Together they looked out along the sheer face of the cliff on either side of the base and the mountains that surrounded them. Greef was already planning their next move. "The reactor should be set in the heat shaft," he said. "If we drain the cooling lines, this whole base will go up in a matter of minutes."

"Look," the Mythrol said, pointing to a nearby armored vehicle. "It's a mint Trexler Marauder. You know how much we can get for this on the black market?"

"And it's gonna be vaporized like the rest of this base," Mando said. "Now let's go." They walked away, past the

Marauder, the Mythrol visibly saddened to see it go.

Inside the base, the monitor displaying the shuttle bay feed suddenly went blank.

The Imperial officer on duty spent a moment blinking at the screen before activating his comm. "Shuttle bay, this is command. Your security feed just went down. Can you check your relay hub?" He paused, waiting for a response. "Shuttle bay? This is—"

An arm wrapped around his throat from behind, pulling him out of the seat, and Cara Dune put the officer to sleep with a smooth choke hold. Mando went to the console while Greef snatched the security key from the downed officer.

"This'll come in handy," he said.

"I found the heat shaft," Mando said. "Let's go."

They took off down the hallway, moving cautiously, avoiding troopers as they went. Rounding the corner, the Mandalorian pointed at the door leading to the reactor. "There, Mythrol. Slice that door."

"Use the code cylinder," Greef said, passing him the access key. The Mythrol inserted it into the security port, and an instant later the door slid open to reveal a massive heat shaft. A gantry lined the enormous vertical lava tube. Far below them, lava bubbled orange and red, and carbon flocked every exposed surface, giving the air a sulfuric smell, as if it was leaking up from somewhere underground.

"Whoa," the Mythrol said, staring down.

"Whoa is right." Greef pointed at the narrow platform in front of them that housed the reactor's mechanical board. "That's it. Get on the reactor controls. Drain the cooling lines. We'll watch the doors."

The Mythrol's face lengthened with incredulity. "Me?"

"Yes, you."

"I'm afraid of heights. And heat. And lava. . . ."

"How about if I put you back in carbonite?" Greef snapped. "Get over there!"

The Mythrol stepped out, teetering perilously along the platform, gripping the console for dear life. "There's no guardrail on this—"

"Come on!" Greef said. "Hurry up, hurry up!"

Trembling visibly, the Mythrol edged along the catwalk until he reached the controls. Upon arrival, he managed to steady his nerves enough to type in a series of commands, and the visual display on the command module showed the diagram of the pipes venting coolant, accompanied by an abrupt and unmistakable spike in reactor heat. Everything on the screen went red. Alarms around the base began to shriek.

"All right," the Mythrol said, already scuttling back toward the others. "She's gonna blow. Let's get out of here!"

They ducked through the hatch into the corridor and began running down the hall, dodging another platoon of troopers as they stepped into what Mando realized was some kind of research lab. On either side of the darkened space stood rows of glowing tanks filled with fluid.

But it wasn't just fluid.

Inside them, weird figures floated. Mando saw that they were humanoid in appearance, grotesque and disfigured. The things had faces, their expressions twisted into sightless and terrible shapes.

"What the . . . ?" Greef said.

Cara frowned at him. "I thought you said this was a forward operating base."

"I thought it was," the magistrate said.

"No," she said. "This isn't a military operation. This is a lab. We need to get into the system and figure out what's going on."

"What about the reactor?" the Mythrol asked.

Cara pointed at the nearby workstation. "Do it!"

The Mythrol hurried over, surveying the controls, and activated a recording. A hologram appeared in front of them, and Mando immediately recognized the speaker as Dr. Pershing, the bespectacled scientist who had been serving at the behest of the Empire and Moff Gideon what seemed like a long time ago.

". . . replicated the results of the subsequent trials," Pershing was saying, "which also resulted in catastrophic failure. There were promising effects for an entire fortnight, but then, sadly, the body rejected the blood." His voice was grim. "Unfortunately we have exhausted our initial supply of blood. The Child is small, and I was only able to harvest a limited amount without killing him. If these experiments are to continue as requested, we would again require access to the donor." He paused and drew in a determined breath. "I will not disappoint you again, Moff Gideon."

Mando looked from the hologram to Greef and Cara. "This must be an old transmission," he said. "Moff Gideon is dead."

"No," the Mythrol said. "This recording is three days old."

A wave of concern passed over Mando. "If Gideon's alive—"

"Hold it right there!" someone said behind them. An instant later, a hail of blaster fire erupted in the room.

Cara spun around and fired back, joined by Mando and Greef.

"I need to get the kid," Mando said.

"Jet back," Cara told him. "You're faster that way. We'll head back on the speeder and meet you in town."

Nodding, Mando took off running down the corridor. His path took him back to the heat shaft and up the tunnel. The heat from the reactor was already reaching critical mass as he burst skyward and headed back to town.

He only hoped it wasn't too late.

As they headed for the shuttle pad, Cara, Greef, and the Mythrol found themselves surrounded by troopers. More Imperial reinforcements on speeder bikes surged up the corridor behind them, pinning them down from both sides.

"We're trapped!" the Mythrol said.

"Is that so?" Cara eyed the Marauder, its massive armored flank half-hidden under the tarp draped over it. "Cover me!"

"What does she think she's doing?" the Mythrol asked.

Cara leapt behind the controls of the Marauder. "All right, baby girl," she said, "let's see what you got."

Powering up the vehicle, Cara tore across the landing pad toward Greef and the Mythrol, pulling up alongside them and swinging open the side hatch.

"What are you guys waiting for, an invitation? Let's move!"

Greef continued firing at the Imperial troops. "Go! Go, go, go!" he said. The Mythrol darted for the vehicle, and the magistrate followed, ducking inside. Cara started accelerating toward the tunnel leading into the base, and just as they were about to make it, the heavy door slammed in front of them, blocking their path.

Without hesitation, Cara put the vehicle in reverse and whipped it around. Now they were facing the troopers firing directly at them, and beyond that, the end of the landing pad where nothing but gravity awaited them.

The Mythrol leaned forward, his voice panicky. "You're not seriously considering—"

"Hang on!" Cara said, and rammed the thruster all the way down. The Marauder surged forward and sailed headlong over the edge. The Mythrol and Greef both started screaming. For what felt like a very long and heart-stopping time, the vehicle was in terminal velocity.

It crashed to the canyon floor, crushing the waiting speeder and sending sparks through the air.

"Wait," the Mythrol said, looking around. "Was that my speeder?"

Cara didn't bother answering. They were flying along between razor-sharp spires and rocky outcroppings, and within seconds she realized that they weren't alone. A cluster of Imperial speeder bikes had followed them over the edge and joined the chase, already closing in fast. She pushed the thruster forward harder.

"Man the guns!"

Greef Karga nodded, glad to be of service. "Copy that." He moved into the heavy turret, bringing the Marauder's sophisticated weapons array online. The red targeting screen in front of him showed one of the speeders surging forward into his sights, and he fired off a series of blasts, taking out the bike. "One down!"

It was a good start, but things almost immediately became more complicated. The remaining two Imperial speeder bikes split up and accelerated hard, surging forward to flank the Marauder on either side, out of reach of the vehicle's cannons. The riders began firing from their protected positions, and one of the bikers climbed up the side of the Marauder. To her left, Cara saw the other biker closing in. She swerved hard, flattening the speeder bike and its rider against the canyon wall in an orange burst of flame.

Greef Karga frowned. "Where's the third one?" he asked. Then he saw the trooper on the display screen, standing atop the Marauder with a grenade in his hand. Greef spun the cannons around, pinning the figure in his crosshairs, and pulled the trigger with a chuckle.

A moment later, there was a massive explosion behind them as the base's reactor reached critical mass and finally exploded in a spectacular, ground-shaking fireball that filled the horizon behind them.

"Yes!" the Mythrol said. "We did it!"

Cara smiled. "Headed home, boss."

Suddenly, laser fire tore down from above them. Looking up, they saw TIE fighters closing in.

"I may have been premature," the Mythrol said.

"Take evasive!" Greef shouted. "I got this."

Cara kept going while he engaged the Marauder's ground-to-air targeting display and started lining up the TIE fighter icon in the gunsights. An instant later, the vehicle rocked sideways with the impact of a direct hit.

"What is going on back there?" Cara shouted.

"You wanna come back here and try this?" Greef asked. "Be my guest!"

As the canyon opened up onto the lava flats, all three of the fighters moved downward into targeting position. Behind the weapons array, Greef felt his stomach sinking with a sense of impending doom. There was nowhere left to hide, and it was only a matter of time before the TIEs blew the Marauder to pieces.

"We're almost there!" the Mythrol shouted, but it didn't matter how close they got to the gates of the city if the TIE fighters gunned them down first.

WHOOM! All at once, the fighter behind them erupted in a burst of flame and shrapnel. Cara, Greef, and the Mythrol all looked around to see the ship soaring along behind them.

"Yes!" Greef said, exultant, as they pulled up outside the city gates. "Yes!"

The *Razor Crest* was back.

"Hang on, kid," the Mandalorian said. He took the newly repaired *Razor Crest* through a series of spinning maneuvers and barrel rolls, evading the remaining TIE fighters hot on his tail. Strapped into the jump seat, the Child giggled with delight, snacking on the package of blue cookies he'd brought with him from the classroom.

Mando pushed the ship harder, cutting off one of the fighters and clipping its sail, causing it to trail off to the planet's surface, belching smoke and flame. Pulling back on the flight controls, he took the *Crest* through another series of acrobatic spins. Behind him, the Child was no longer giggling.

The remaining TIE took aim and fired, roaring nearer. Mando corkscrewed into a dive. Snapping the *Crest* around to face the oncoming TIE, he opened fire.

The fighter exploded in front of him, and the Mandalorian drew back on the yoke.

"Not too bad, huh, kid?"

The Child looked at him and spit up a glut of blue-colored goo down his own chest.

Greef Karga's voice came through the comm. "That was some pretty impressive flying, Mando. What do I owe you?"

The Mandalorian set the ship on autopilot and leaned over to clean off the Child's cloak. "With the repairs, let's call it even."

"Can I at least buy you a drink?"

"Sorry," Mando said, still wiping at the stain, "I have some, uh, onboard maintenance I gotta take care of. Then we gotta hit the road before Gideon catches wise."

"Well," Greef said, "good luck flying, my friend."

Mando settled back behind the controls and prepared to jump to hyperspace. He'd taken the last of the Child's cookies, and the Child didn't seem to mind.

For once, he didn't look hungry.

Aboard the bridge of the Imperial light cruiser, a communications officer was speaking to a hologram of a Mimbanese worker from the Nevarro landing fields, her voice hushed and urgent. "What do you have for me?"

"The device has been planted as you requested," the worker replied.

"Good," the officer said. "You will be well rewarded in the new era."

She ended the communication and walked off the bridge, down the corridor, and past soldiers and officers to a large bay. Moff Gideon stood with his back to her, surveying the rows of shiny black metal armor along either wall.

"Moff Gideon."

He turned to look at the officer.

"The tracking beacon has been installed on the *Razor Crest*."

Gideon's lips tightened ever so slightly. "Does he still have the asset?"

"Yes," the officer said. "Our source confirmed it."

Gideon gazed back at the rows of black armor with a frown. "And we will be ready."

CHAPTER 13

CLANG! CLANG! CLANG!

The oblong iron bell rang out through the smoky night air, sounding the alarm. Outside the city, the gates swung open and guards emerged into the darkness, blasters at the ready. There was no radio chatter between them. They all knew what was happening.

She was there.

Somewhere in the darkness, the lone figure appeared to drift almost weightlessly through a burned landscape where skeletal remnants of trees stood silent vigil. A mist created by the heat of the land hung over the ground as the guards made their way forward, weapons at the ready. The guards were well trained and heavily armed.

It didn't make a bit of difference.

The figure spun, dodging blaster fire and lashing

out with the lightsabers she held in either hand. One of the blades cut a chunk from a nearby tree branch, and she reached out with the Force, propelling the slab of wood toward a nearby guard. By the time the others had a chance to react, it was too late. Ahsoka Tano had already vanished again, only to reappear in silence to attack the guards whose sensors had never detected her movement.

High above the wall, the magistrate of Calodan gazed down at the woods with a scowl of contempt. Next to her, the captain of the guard, a mercenary named Lang, stood at attention. They both watched and listened to pulses of blaster fire and screams from the seething woods below.

Then it was silent.

Stepping to the edge, the magistrate spoke. "Show yourself," she called out. "Jedi."

Silence from the mists. Then Ahsoka stepped forward, lightsabers blazing to life at her sides. Her orange skin was illustrated with symmetrical white facial markings on her forehead and cheeks. Instead of hair, she had hornlike montrals and head-tails that hung over her shoulders and down her back. They were striped white and blue to the tips.

For a long moment, she didn't move. Instead of anger,

her face showed a composure unified by elegance and a warrior's confidence.

"I've been expecting you," the magistrate said.

Ahsoka's voice was as calm as her face. "Then you know what I want," she said.

"You will learn nothing from me." The magistrate signaled to her left. From the shadows, an HK droid brought forth a manacled citizen, shoving the man toward the edge of the precipice. "How many lives is the knowledge I possess worth to you?" the magistrate asked.

Ahsoka said nothing.

"One?" the magistrate continued. "Ten? How about a hundred?" She waited, but no answer came. "The lives of these citizens mean nothing to me. Now, because of you, these people will suffer."

"They already suffer under your rule," Ahsoka said. "Surrender, or face the consequences." She raised one of the lightsabers, pointing its tip up at the magistrate. "You have one day to decide."

She switched off the lightsabers and was gone. The night air fell still again. Up on the wall, Lang turned to face the magistrate.

"We will be ready when she returns," Lang promised.

If the magistrate heard him, she gave no indication. Turning to the droid who'd accompanied the citizen, she raised a dismissive hand. "Cage him," she said, and walked away, leaving Lang to gaze out at the scorched forest and whatever awaited him out there.

High above Corvus, the *Razor Crest* emerged out of hyperspace and began its steady descent. In the cockpit, Mando and the Child gazed down at the shining planet rising into view before them.

"Corvus," Mando said. "This is the place." He activated the *Crest*'s landing cycle. "I've detected a beacon. You better get back in your seat."

The Child was looking at the metal ball screwed onto the top of one of the ship's shifter controls.

"Hey, what did I tell you? Back in your seat."

Reluctantly, the Child crawled back behind Mando to the jump seat, onto his booster cushion. Mando brought the ship in low, descending through a cloud layer thick with soot and smoke. Something terrible had happened there, burning the land to a cinder and staining the air a contaminated shade of yellowish brown.

Mando passed over the outer stone of the spaceport and brought the ship down for a landing in a clearing amid the scorched trees. Extending the rear ramp, he walked down and saw the Child trundling along behind him, clutching something in one tiny hand. After a moment Mando realized it was the silver shifter knob from the ship's controls.

"What did I say about that?" he said. "This needs to stay in the ship." Turning and sticking the silver knob into his pocket, he peered through the blackened landscape to the wall in the distance. "Not much to see out here. Never had dealings with a Jedi before. Let's head into town, see if we can pick up a lead."

With the kid tucked into a pouch at his side, he set off for the city gates.

◆

"State your business," a voice spoke from the top of the wall.

Mando raised his head to look up at the man standing there. He had a coldness about him, his expression telling Mando that he was a man whose authority there went unchallenged, especially by strangers. Armed droids flanked him on either side.

"Been tracking for a few days," Mando said. "Looking for a layover."

"Nice armor," the man said. "You a hunter then?"

"That's right."

"Guild?"

Mando nodded. "Last I checked."

There was a pause. "Open the gate," the man said.

Mando went inside. The streets of Corvus were hushed and grim. Compared with the thriving city on Nevarro, everything about this place felt fearful and depressed. Townspeople slumped on the sidewalk, not bothering to glance up as Mando passed, or if they did, they quickly crept down alleyways, retreating into the shadows. Approaching a vendor with a table of cooked meats, Mando tried to catch the merchant's attention.

"Pardon me, vendor, have you heard of anyone pa—"

Without a word, the vendor turned and hurried away. Continuing along, Mando saw a man standing with two children. "You there," he said, "I need some information. I'm looking for someone."

The man gestured for the children to leave, then addressed the Mandalorian in a hushed voice. "Please, do not speak to them, or to any of us."

"Look," Mando said, "I just need to know—"

"The magistrate wants to see you," said someone behind him.

Mando turned to see two heavily armed guards waiting there. As they escorted him toward the inner gate, Mando saw more citizens standing on either side of the path. They were prisoners, forced to remain motionless on platforms surrounded by metal rings that crackled and snapped with high-voltage current. They groaned and cried out in pain and fatigue. They pleaded with Mando as he passed.

"Help us," one of the citizens managed.

"She'll kill us all," murmured another.

Mando stepped through the passageway to the inner courtyard beyond. The air was fresh and clean. A low stone bridge stretched across a calm reflecting pool surrounded by lush greenery and thriving life. Standing on the bridge, a woman dressed in magisterial robes scattered flakes of food for the fish in the pond. Her face was cool and imperious, the features honed by cruelty.

"Come forward," she said.

Mando approached, and she spoke without bothering to look at him.

"You are a Mandalorian?"

"Yes," he said.

"I have a proposition that may interest you."

"My price is high."

The magistrate finished feeding the fish and turned her full attention to him. "The target is priceless," she said. "A Jedi plagues me. I want you to kill her."

"That's a difficult task."

"One that you are well suited for," the magistrate said. "The Jedi are the ancient enemy of Mandalore."

Mando made no move to go closer. "As I said, my price is high."

Signaling the droid behind her, the magistrate waited while it brought forward a long silver spear, then placed it in her hand. She turned and gave it to Mando.

"What do you make of this?"

He hefted it, feeling its weight, then struck it against his gauntlet, listening to the unmistakable ring of metal against metal, the same musical tone he'd heard many times in the forge of the Armorer on Nevarro. He looked up at the magistrate. "Beskar."

She smiled, enjoying his reaction. "Pure beskar, like your armor. Kill the Jedi, and it's yours."

Mando stared at her and felt the Child stirring uncomfortably in the pouch at his side. He returned the spear to the magistrate.

"Where do I find this Jedi?" he asked.

CHAPTER 14

WALKING OUT through the gates into the glow of the smog-yellowed sky, Mando was aware of the captain of the guard, the man called Lang, looking down at the Child in his pouch.

"What is that thing?" Lang scowled.

"I keep it around for luck," Mando said.

"You're gonna need it, where you're headed." Lang stood watching as the Mandalorian set out. Then the captain of the guard turned and went back into the village, closing the gates behind him.

Mando walked into the forest, rifle slung over his shoulder, making his way across the steaming landscape amid charred tree trunks that stood like soldiers of a forgotten war.

Something shifted in the forest behind him.

Mando stopped, glancing down at the Child. "You

hear that?" Then, after listening a moment, he put the Child down and unslung his rifle. "Sit right here. Let me see what's out there." Removing the scope, he studied the surroundings but saw nothing. "False alarm."

The attack came from above. A gray-cloaked figure swept down from the mists, slashing with brilliant white blades. Instinctively Mando raised one beskar-armored forearm in front of his face, blocking the blow that otherwise would've ended the fight in a single stroke.

His assailant moved faster, swinging both lightsabers, the blades clanging off his armor. Thrusting one arm forward, Mando blasted her with his flamethrower, and she spun away, using the cloak to protect herself. He fired his grappling line, ensnaring her, but before he could finish the battle, she leapt into the air, taking the line with her and sailing over a tree branch to pull Mando off his feet.

Using the vibroblade from his boot, Mando severed the line. At the same moment, his opponent slashed herself free, and they both dropped to the ground simultaneously, recovering quickly. Mando's blaster was already pointed at her, and she had angled her blades into a defensive stance.

"Ahsoka Tano!" Mando said. "Bo-Katan sent me. We need to talk."

She gazed at him for a moment . . . and then beyond him, then disengaged her lightsabers. "I hope it's about him," she said.

Mando turned to look where she was staring and saw the Child sitting on a rock, watching them. Ahsoka approached him with quiet wonder, the two of them regarding each other with what almost seemed like mutual recognition.

It was night.

Ahsoka had taken Mando and the Child to a place of safety between large moss-covered stones and bent trees. A thin stream trickled between the stones, which were carved with ancient inscriptions, weathered and worn away by time. She and the Child sat with a lantern between them as Mando waited and paced restlessly, occasionally looking over at them silhouetted in the moonlight. He could hear the faint noises of the Child in the distance.

At last they came over to where he was waiting. Ahsoka sat down on a large tree that had gained purchase in the flat stone and overhung the creek below. In the stillness, Mando could hear the gurgle of water.

"Is he speaking?" he asked. "Do you understand him?"

"In a way," she said. "Grogu and I can feel each other's thoughts."

"Grogu?"

"Yes. That's his name."

"Grogu," Mando repeated, seeing how the kid perked up at the sound of his name.

"He was raised at the Jedi Temple on Coruscant," Ahsoka said. "Many Masters trained him over the years. At the end of the Clone Wars when the Empire rose to power, he was hidden. Someone took him from the Temple. Then his memory becomes dark. He seemed alone, lost."

Ahsoka watched Grogu looking at Mando, seeing how fond he was of the bounty hunter who'd become his protector and caregiver.

"I've only known one other being like this," she continued, "a wise Jedi Master named Yoda. Can he still wield the Force?"

"You mean his powers?" Mando asked.

Ahsoka smiled. "The Force is what gives him his powers. It is an energy field created by all living things. To wield it takes a great deal of training and discipline."

"I've seen him do things I can't explain," Mando said.

Ahsoka regarded little Grogu, who had tucked his

head down and drifted off to sleep sitting between them.

"My task was to bring him to a Jedi," Mando said.

"The Jedi Order fell a long time ago."

"So did the Empire," Mando said, "yet it still hunts him. He needs your help."

Ahsoka was still looking at Grogu, his lowered face aglow in the firelight. "Let him sleep," she said. "I'll test him in the morning."

At dawn, Mando carried Grogu along the side of the creek to meet Ahsoka. They stopped near the top of a hill where the sun seemed to be shining a little brighter through the fog, and he set the Child down in front of her.

"Let's see what knowledge is lurking inside that little mind," Ahsoka said. She picked up a small smooth stone and held it up, moving her hand gently. A moment later, Mando saw the stone rising from her palm. With a gesture, she moved the stone forward, floating it across the distance between herself and Grogu, who raised his little hand to receive it with a coo of delight.

"Now," Ahsoka said, "return the stone to me, Grogu."

The Child didn't move. He seemed to be struggling.

"The stone, Grogu."

Still struggling, the Child made a faint grunting

sound and tossed the stone on the ground, then sank down, silent and sad.

"I sense much fear in you," Ahsoka said, and glanced at Mando. "He's hidden his abilities to survive over the years." She paused, reflecting. "Let's try something else. Come over here."

Grogu didn't budge. "He's stubborn," Mando said.

"Not him," Ahsoka said, "you."

"Me?"

"I want to see if he'll listen to you."

"That would be a first," Mando said.

Ahsoka smiled faintly. "I like firsts," she said. "Good or bad, they're always memorable. Now"—she gestured—"hold the stone out in the palm of your hand."

With some skepticism, Mando bent down and picked up the stone. Almost immediately Grogu's ears perked up, and he became more interested now that his guardian was involved in the game.

"Tell him to lift it up," Ahsoka said.

"All right, kid," Mando said. "Lift the stone."

"Grogu," Ahsoka prompted softly.

With a sigh, Mando tried again. "Grogu, come on. Take the stone."

Grogu tilted his head, ears perked up, but he seemed more interested in the Mandalorian than the stone.

"You see?" Mando said. "I told you he's stubborn."

"Try to connect with him," Ahsoka said.

Mando drew in a deep breath. The kid was still gazing at him hopefully, fondly. Finally Mando reached into his belt pouch and pulled out the shiny shifter knob he'd taken from the Child at the landing site. He held it out in the palm of his hand as he had the stone. Grogu's eyes gleamed at the sight of the metal ball.

"Grogu, do you want this?"

Grogu reached out with one little hand. Mando was aware of Ahsoka watching intently.

"Well, go ahead," he said. "That's right, take it. Come on. You can have it."

Hand still outstretched, Grogu pulled the ball from Mando's palm and brought it flying toward him so it landed neatly within his own grasp.

"Good job!" Mando said. "Good job, kid! You see that? That's right. I knew you could do it. Very good."

Grogu clutched the knob, beaming with the pleasure of the new toy and the Mandalorian's praise. But when Mando looked at Ahsoka, she was not smiling.

"He's formed a strong attachment to you," she said. "I cannot train him."

"*What?*" Mando asked. "Why not? You've seen what he can do."

"His attachment to you makes him vulnerable to his fears, his anger."

"All the more reason to train him."

"No," she said firmly. "I've seen what such feelings can do to a fully trained Jedi Knight, to the best of us. I will not start this child down that path." Her voice lowered sadly. "Better to let his abilities fade." She put on her cloak and prepared to leave. "I've delayed too long. I must get back to the village."

As she walked off, Mando called after her. "The magistrate sent me to kill you."

Ahsoka stopped in her tracks, turned, and looked back. Grogu was sitting between them, his eyes moving back and forth, following the conversation intently.

"I didn't agree to anything," Mando said. "And I'll help you with your problem, if you see to it that Grogu is properly trained."

The Jedi didn't respond, but the expression on her face, uncertainty mingled with hope, gave him all the answer he needed.

Picking up Grogu, he moved to join her.

CHAPTER 15

AS THEY WALKED THROUGH the misty landscape, Mando filled in Ahsoka on what he'd already discovered about the magistrate from the short amount of time he'd been inside the city walls. "She has a small army of guards armed with A-350 blaster rifles, two HK-87 assassin droids, and a hired gunfighter." He thought about Lang, the man who'd escorted him through the gates and into the forest. "He reads ex-military to me. Combined, not even your laser swords would be able to protect you from all that firepower."

"True," Ahsoka said, "but don't underestimate the magistrate, either."

"Who is she?" Mando asked. "She offered me a staff of pure beskar to kill you."

"Morgan Elsbeth," Ahsoka said. "During the Clone Wars her people were massacred. She survived and let her anger fuel an industry which helped build the Imperial starfleet. She plundered worlds, destroying them in the process."

Mando gazed at the scorched forest. "Looks like she's still in business."

"When you were in the city, did you see any prisoners?"

"I saw three villagers strung up just outside the inner gate," Mando said.

"We must find a way to free them."

Mando considered it for a moment. "A Mandalorian and a Jedi? They'll never see it coming."

◈

They didn't.

At dusk, the guards along the city wall peered into the haze, toward the distant tree line. When a cloaked figure passed through the shadows, the guard at the gate jerked his head upward. "It's her. Sound the alarm!"

The oblong iron bell began ringing out, but its tolling didn't last long. From below, Ahsoka sprang to the top of the wall, lightsabers ignited. Caught completely by surprise, the soldiers fired wildly, but Ahsoka slipped between them unharmed, attacking with her blades, disarming them and knocking one of them over the edge. The guard holding the iron mallet to strike the bell swung it at her. Dodging the mallet, Ahsoka whirled around and sliced through the mallet and the iron bell itself, sending it in two separate pieces over the edge and into the street below with an earsplitting crash.

Inside the wall, villagers and guards rushed around in a flurry of activity in response to the attack. Moments later, the inner gate swung open and the magistrate emerged, followed by Lang and her two droid guardians. She strode past her other guards to the front of the group and gazed down the street toward the toppled bell.

Then she stopped.

At the far end of the street, Ahsoka Tano stepped into view. The magistrate stared at her. For a moment neither one moved. The breeze made the lanterns that hung overhead sway back and forth, casting restless shadows on the guards on either side.

Ahsoka began walking toward her. As the guards raised their weapons, the magistrate signaled for them to remain calm. Twenty meters away, Ahsoka stopped and removed something from her belt, tossing it on the ground in front of the magistrate, where it landed with a clang. Looking down, the magistrate saw that it was a piece of the Mandalorian's armor.

"Your bounty hunter failed," Ahsoka said.

The magistrate said nothing.

"Tell me what I want to know," Ahsoka said. "Where is your master?"

The magistrate turned to Lang. "Kill her."

"Love to," Lang said. Raising his scatterblaster, he pulled the trigger, firing a volley of lasers at Ahsoka. But the Jedi was already leaping into the air, vaulting over the scattershot, and landing on top of the roof of an adjacent building. Guards fired up at her from below, and Ahsoka deflected the blasts with her lightsabers before turning and racing across the rooftop into the darkness.

"I'll take care of this," Lang said.

The magistrate gestured toward the droids. "Take them with you." After Lang and the HKs had departed, she turned and started back through the inner wall. On her way, she spoke to the two guards standing by the inner gate and gestured to the caged prisoners. "Execute them, then go door to door."

When she was gone, the two guards raised their blasters, aiming at the caged prisoners. "Please, don't!" one of them cried out, but before the guards could fire, a sudden whine of jet pack rockets shrieked down from above. The Mandalorian landed, kicking one of the guards aside, then spun around with his blaster raised, firing on the other. He stopped, seeing the man who'd been with the two children in the street the day before.

Mando nodded at him, and he and the man moved toward the first cage to begin freeing the prisoners.

Lang made his way down the darkened side street, scatterblaster at the ready, in pursuit of the Jedi. He was not afraid. Remaining calm and focused would give him the best advantage he could hope for.

In the distance, he heard the sizzling hiss of a light-saber, and a guard screamed. Lang turned and moved in the direction of the scream, but by the time he arrived, the fight was already over. The bodies of guards lay crumpled in a pile.

From the corner of his eye, Lang caught a flicker of movement on the rooftop. Pivoting, he fired up at the Jedi. Despite the whirling lightsabers, she couldn't deflect the spray of the scatterblaster. As she fled down the alley, Lang gestured at the droids. "Get up there!"

The droids climbed up on the rooftop, and Lang moved forward, edging around the corner, down another alley, and into an open main street, stalking Ahsoka on the ground.

Lang could smell blood.

It wouldn't be long.

Inside the inner courtyard, the magistrate was waiting.

She stood on the stone path that divided the pool of water, the beskar spear resting on her shoulder.

After evading the droids and slipping over the courtyard wall, Ahsoka Tano stood at the other end of the stone path, just inside the closed gates. The lightsabers in her hands ignited, their blazing white blades reflected in the pool below.

The magistrate strode forward with composure and purpose. She raised the spear and moved it into a defensive position, countering Ahsoka's stance. The two women sized each other up, eyeing their opponent for weaknesses.

Then they struck.

Beskar and blade clashed as the two opponents fought, lunging, thrusting, and parrying, the tranquil surface of the water reflecting the blur of combat above. Spinning the spear, the magistrate knocked aside one of Ahsoka's blades and went in for the kill. Ahsoka blocked the attack with her other saber. At the last second she reversed her grip and used her other hand to grab the spear from the magistrate's grasp. In less than a second, the blade of the lightsaber was at the magistrate's neck, centimeters from the pulsing veins of her throat.

While Ahsoka was scaling the wall into the magistrate's courtyard, Mando looked down the street and saw Lang approaching.

"So you threw in with the Jedi," Lang said.

Mando gazed back at him. "Looks that way," he said. In the distance they could hear the clang of lightsabers and beskar, the grunts and cries of the duel inside the inner courtyard.

"Who do you think's gonna win?" Lang asked. "Could be your side . . . could be my side." He began to advance slowly toward Mando. "I got no quarrel with you, Mandalorian."

Mando raised one hand. "That's far enough," he said. His other hand went down to the blaster holstered on his right hip, fingers open, waiting.

"You and I, we're a lot alike," Lang said. "Willing to lay our lives down for the right cause." He gestured with a nod in the direction of the battle. "Which this is not."

In the silence, they heard the unmistakable sound of beskar hitting the ground. Lang's face was unsurprised.

"Sounds like you win," he said, and slowly bent forward to lay down his scatterblaster.

Then, unexpectedly, at the last second, he whipped out his pistol.

ZZAACHOW!

The blaster in Mando's hand fired a single round, but that was all he needed. Lang flew backward and landed in the street, motionless.

Mando holstered his blaster and turned away.

◆

The next day, for the first time in recent memory, there was rejoicing in the streets of Calodan. People cheered, flying colorful banners and flags up and down the public areas and plazas. The sense of relief and celebration was palpable, even as Mando and Ahsoka walked through the gates and out toward the forest beyond.

"I believe this was your payment," she said, offering him the spear.

"No," the Mandalorian said. "I can't accept. I didn't finish the job."

"No," she said, "but this belongs with a Mandalorian."

He took it from her with a nod of gratitude.

"Where is your little friend?" Ahsoka asked.

"Back at the ship," Mando said. In the silence that followed, he realized this might be the last time he got to see Grogu. "Wait here. I'll go get him."

He found the kid in his hammock aboard the *Crest*, fast asleep. Mando watched him for a moment. Grogu stirred in his sleep, frowning a little. Mando took hold of the hammock and rocked it gently. "Wake up, buddy," he said softly. "It's time to say goodbye."

Grogu opened his eyes sleepily and made a little cooing sound as Mando bundled him up and tucked him into the crook of his arm, a gesture that had become second nature. As he carried him down the rear ramp, he saw Ahsoka waiting.

"You're like a father to him," Ahsoka said, standing amid the charred trees. "I cannot train him."

At the end of the ramp, Mando stopped. "You made me a promise, and I held up my end."

She paused, considering. "There is one possibility," she said. "Go to the planet Tython. There you will find the ancient ruins of a temple that has a strong connection to the Force. Place Grogu on the seeing stone at the top of the mountain."

"Then what?" Mando asked.

"Then Grogu may choose his path," she said. "If he reaches out through the Force there's a chance that a Jedi may sense his presence and come searching for him. Then again, there aren't many Jedi left."

"Thank you," Mando said, hearing the sincerity in her words. The Child made a soft noise and clung to Mando's arms.

"May the Force be with you," Ahsoka said.

Nodding, the Mandalorian turned and carried Grogu back aboard the ship. Moments later the *Crest's* engines roared to life. Ahsoka watched as the flare of engines washed over her. Then she turned and began to walk back through the burned forest toward the city.

CHAPTER 16

"GROGU," MANDO SAID.

In the jump seat of the *Razor Crest*, where he'd been happily playing with the little metal ball, the Child sat up and chirped at the sound of his name. The Mandalorian chuckled. The kid returned his attention to the ball, grunting softly as he turned it over in his hands.

"Grogu," Mando said again, and the Child glanced at him again. Mando laughed. The name was definitely growing on him. "Give me the ball." He reached over and held out his hand. "Grogu, give me the ball. Come on."

After a moment, Grogu reluctantly gave him the knob. Mando held it away from him, then opened his hand. "Okay," he said. "Here we go. You can have it, just like before." The Child peered at him, head cocked, ears stretched out. "Grogu, you can have it. Come on."

Grogu stretched out one hand, eyes closing slightly in focused concentration. Mando felt the ball twitching slightly, and then suddenly it leapt from his hand and flew back to the kid. *"Dank farrik!"* Mando said with delight.

Grogu stared at him, taken aback by Mando's reaction, fearful that he'd done something wrong.

"Hey, no, no," Mando said. "I'm not mad at you. You did good. I just . . ." He hesitated, searching for the words. "When the nice lady said you had training, I just . . ." He shook his head. "You're special, kid."

Grogu began to smile, understanding. As the Child continued to play with the little metal toy, Mando focused his attention on the ship and the destination ahead of them.

"We're gonna find you that place you belong," he said, "and they're gonna take real good care of you." Gazing at the planet appearing through the windscreen, he set the controls to begin their descent. "This is Tython. That's where we're gonna try to find you a Jedi." He glanced over at Grogu again. "But you have to agree to go with them if they want you to, understand? Plus I can't train you. You're too powerful. Don't you want to learn more of that Jedi stuff?"

Grogu made a small snorting noise, his attention still focused on the ball.

"I agreed to take you back to your own kind," Mando said, speaking as much to himself as to the Child. "So that's what I need to do. You understand, right?"

Grogu looked at him. Mando stared down at the planet and continued his descent. He could see the hilly terrain approaching, a verdant landscape of vegetation and growth. Amid it all, a sharp outcropping of ancient stones came into view, arranged in a circle, with one very distinct stone in the center.

"Looks like that's the magic rock I'm supposed to take you down to." Examining the stones, angled vertically so they came together at the top of the peak, he shook his head. "Sorry, buddy. I can't land on the top. Too small. Looks like we're gonna have to travel the last stretch with the windows down."

Moments later they were soaring over the mountaintops, Grogu wrapped in the Mandalorian's arm. Grogu wore a delighted expression, his ears flapping in the wind as Mando's jet pack carried them to the stone formation.

They landed on the hilltop and walked over to the henge for a closer look. The tall rocks cast long shadows around them as Mando carried Grogu into the middle. Upon closer examination, the bounty hunter saw that the center stone was inscribed with eroded petroglyphs and ancient carvings whose meanings he couldn't begin to interpret.

"Well, I guess this is it," Mando said. "Does this look 'Jedi' to you?"

Grogu gazed up at him blankly.

Lifting Grogu up, Mando placed him on the center stone—the seeing stone, as Ahsoka had called it. "I guess you sit right here. Okay, here we go."

Grogu cooed and cocked his head curiously, still looking at Mando, as if expecting him to do something.

"This is the seeing stone," Mando prompted. "Are you seeing anything?" He began to walk around the stone, switching on the optical enhancements in his visor to investigate the area. "Or are they supposed to see you?"

But there were no answers there. Returning his gaze to Grogu, he saw the Child had become distracted by a butterfly that had fluttered over to him. Mando sighed. "Oh, come on, kid. Ahsoka told me all I had to do is get you here and you'd do the rest—"

From overhead came the whine of an approaching engine. Mando looked up, tracking the unfamiliar ship as it arced downward across the blue expanse and set-tled in for a landing. Turning toward the arrangement of rocks, he started moving back to the seeing stone.

"Time's up, kid. We gotta get out of here—"

He stopped. On top of the stone, Grogu had closed his eyes. The petroglyphs inscribed around him had begun to glow, sending strange, semi-translucent ten-drils of blue light rising around him.

"We don't have time for this!" Mando said, reaching forward. "We gotta get—"

Wham! He flew backward, repulsed by some invis-ible force, and landed on the ground. Mando leapt up, but Grogu didn't seem to have noticed. His eyes were still shut.

"Hey!" Mando shouted. "Snap out of it! We gotta get out of here!"

Still no response from Grogu. Whatever state he'd entered into, the effect only seemed to be deepening. Blue patterns of light rose more thickly, rippling up from the stone to surround the Child and rising skyward in a strange cylinder of pure energy.

Mando switched on his visor and glanced back at the ship that had just landed, making out the shape of its passenger, a cloaked figure, descending the ramp in the distance. Drawing his blaster, he turned back to Grogu.

"I'll see if I can buy us some time," he said. "Can you please hurry up?"

Without waiting for an answer, Mando began running down the path, footsteps silent as he made his way over uneven terrain, slowing as he got nearer to the ship.

A sudden volley of blaster shots slammed into the ground in front of him, stopping him in his tracks. Mando ducked behind a rock, peering outward.

"I've been tracking you, Mandalorian," said someone with a cold voice.

Mando gazed at the cloaked shape outlined against the blue sky, a pair of weapons strapped to his back. "Are you Jedi?" he asked.

There was no reply.

"Or are you after the Child?"

The figure drew nearer and swept back his hood to expose his face. He was older than Mando had expected, bald and weathered-looking. He made no move to unsling the rifle or gaffi stick from their straps on his back, leaving himself surprisingly vulnerable.

"I'm here for the armor," the man said.

Mando rose, pointing his blaster. "If you want my armor, you'll have to peel it off my dead body."

The man smiled slightly. "I don't want *your* armor," he said. "I want my armor that you got from Cobb Vanth back on Tatooine. It belongs to me."

"Are you Mandalorian?"

"My name is Boba Fett," the man said. "I'm a simple man making his way through the galaxy, like my father before me."

"Did you take the Creed?"

"I give my allegiance to no one," Fett said.

"The beskar belongs to the Mandalorians," Mando said. "It was looted from us during the Purge."

Fett was unmoved. "The armor was my father's," he said. "Now it's mine."

"What's to stop me from dropping you where you stand?"

"Because," Fett said, "I have a sharpshooter up on that ridge with a locked scope that will unload by the time my body hits the ground."

"I'm the one wearing beskar," Mando said. He powered up the weapons array on his wrist gauntlet, preparing to discharge the whistling birds. "As soon as I see that muzzle flash, you're both dead."

"I didn't mean she was going to shoot you," Fett said.

"My friend's locked on to that little companion of yours up on the henge." He pointed up at Grogu, barely visible in the glowing Jedi stone arrangement at the top of the hill. Mando raised his eyes to the ridge, where a figure lay prone on her belly, rifle at the ready.

"And if you remember," the woman called down, "I don't miss."

Mando recognized the voice immediately. "Fennec?"

Fennec Shand peered down at him without taking her finger from the trigger of the sniper rifle. "You have a keen ear, Mando."

"You point that gun away from the kid," Mando said, "or I'll drop you both where you stand."

Boba Fett remained calm. "Let's all put down our weapons and have a chat," he said. "There's no need for bloodshed."

Mando jerked his head in the direction of Fennec. "Tell her to drop the gun."

"After you put down the jet pack," Fett said.

"Same time."

Fett signaled Fennec. "Stand down," he said.

As Mando unclipped his jet pack and rested it on the rocks, Fennec made her way down from the ridge to join the other two. She removed her helmet, enjoying the look of surprise on Mando's face.

"You look like you've just seen a ghost," she said.

"You were dead."

"She was left for dead on the sands of Tatooine," Fett said, "as was I. But fate sometimes steps in to rescue the wretched."

"In my case," Fennec said, "Boba Fett was that fate." She opened her waistcoat to reveal a layer of cybernetic mech in the place where she'd been shot. "And now I am at his service."

"I want my armor back," Fett said.

Mando held the man's gaze. "It goes against the Mandalorian Creed."

"The armor was given to my father, Jango, by your forebears," Fett said. "In exchange I guarantee the safety of the Child, as well as your own."

"The bounty on your little friend has risen significantly," Fennec said. "You can buy ten suits of armor for the price on its head."

Fett nodded. "I'd say we're offering a fair deal under the circumstances."

Mando was about to reply when the shadow of a newly arrived ship glided over them. He looked up to see an Imperial transport landing in the clearing near the *Razor Crest*. Mando reacted instantly, running up the hillside to get Grogu, while Fett and Fennec scrambled down into the rocks below.

"Time to go, kid!" Mando said, reaching the hill where Grogu still sat on the seeing stone, oblivious to everything going on around him. Trying to force his way through the energy field, Mando devoted every ounce of strength he had to pushing his arms in to grab the Child—only to have it shoot him backward again.

For a moment he lay in a heap, dazed, trying to shake it off.

Then he heard the blaster fire.

CHAPTER 17

OF THE FIRST half dozen stormtroopers that poured out of the transport, almost none survived thirty seconds on the ground.

Fennec and Fett began firing down on them immediately. Shooting from an elevated position with the sun behind them, they had every advantage as they picked off the troopers coming down the transport's ramp. Side by side, without a word of communication between them, they took out the first wave, and then Fett gestured silently to his partner before making his move to flank the next squad of troopers. Fennec nodded and disappeared into the bushes and scrub, as silent as a specter.

Down in a clearing at the base of the hill, a group of troopers had set up a tripod cannon and started laying down suppressing fire in an attempt to cover the others, who were making their way up the hill. "Flank left and from above!" the commander ordered.

"Sir, there's too much fire!"

The commander gestured. "Flank them, you idiot!"

Before the protesting trooper could reply, one of Fennec's rifle blasts took him out with a clean shot.

"Up top!" the commander ordered. "Get up there! Get up—"

THWACK! A gaffi stick whipped in from behind him, smashing the commander hard enough to crack his helmet wide open and send him tumbling down the hillside. As the other troopers took notice, Boba Fett stepped in, raising the stick for another attack. He wielded the weapon with a mixture of agility and brute force, taking out the troopers and dropping them to the rocks below.

Up above, Fennec found herself pinned behind a large boulder by the assault of Imperial firepower. A direct hit from the cannon below slammed into the boulder, and she felt it loosening in front of her.

Leaning back for leverage, Fennec bent her knees, propped her feet against the boulder, and began rocking it forward until finally the thing broke loose and rolled down the hillside, picking up speed and crushing the troopers unlucky enough to be in its path. At the bottom of the ravine, the trooper manning the tripod-mounted laser cannon continued firing at the boulder right up until the moment it flattened him.

But the flush of victory was short-lived. In the distance she saw a second Imperial transport swooping down to dispense reinforcements.

I can't keep this up forever, Fennec thought, and a moment later, as if reading her mind, the voice of a trooper rang out from below, and too late, she realized she was surrounded.

"Give yourselves up! We don't want you. We want the Child."

There was a burst of flame, and the trooper jerked backward and collapsed. Looking behind her, Fennec saw the Mandalorian standing on a low rock with his blaster drawn. He'd activated the whistling birds again, and this time he'd released them. The tiny guided missiles had swarmed the troopers' ranks, tearing through them and dropping the nearest ones.

"Okay," Mando said, "let's move in."

Advancing forward, weapons raised, they stood back to back, firing into the next wave of Imperial troops at point-blank range. Every shot was a direct hit, but for every trooper they took out, more took their place. Within moments they were being flanked and encircled.

"This isn't looking good," Fennec said.

"I've seen worse." Mando kept firing, taking out another trooper. "You can get out of here. I owe you for last time."

She shook her head. "We have a deal."

Mando didn't like their odds. Even fighting together, they were already badly outnumbered. He found himself wondering what would happen to Grogu if he and Fennec didn't make it out. How long would the energy field protect the Child from the Imperials who had come for him?

As the surrounding troopers moved closer, a detonator dropped out of the sky, landing squarely among their ranks and blowing them backward. The shockwave was disorienting and sent the other troopers scrambling as the armored figure who'd thrown the explosive swooped down via jet pack to land among them.

Boba Fett had recovered his armor.

The man attacked with speed and ferocity, advancing forward, blasting troopers, and engaging hand-to-hand with the ones he didn't shoot. Their blasters pinged harmlessly off the beskar. Deploying close-range projectiles from his belt, he kept attacking until the last of the troopers whirled around and started their retreat.

"Back to the ship!" one of them shrieked in thinly veiled panic. "Back to the ship!"

Scrambling up the ramp, the last Imperials barely made it inside before the transports dusted off to speed skyward. Fett watched them go for a moment, then switched on the target stalk on his helmet and leaned forward. A guided missile sailed through the air, arcing up to strike one of the transports, which promptly exploded and fell into the second. Both ships erupted in one colossal fireball, and the wreckage fell out of the sky, into the mountain range below.

"Nice shot," Mando said.

"I was aiming for the other one," Fett replied.

Then out of nowhere, an energy blast was fired down from the sky. It hit the *Razor Crest* with pinpoint accuracy, obliterating the ship and enveloping it in a plume of smoke and flame, leaving nothing but a blackened crater.

Mando stood frozen, unable to speak, staring at the place where his ship had been. It was Fennec who broke the silence, turning to Boba Fett. "Better get to your ship."

Unhesitating, Fett activated his jet pack and lifted off. Mando was still staring at the smoking ruin of the *Razor Crest*. Turning his gaze upward, he used the visor to search the sky in the direction of the energy blast and saw the shape of an Imperial light cruiser high above.

Something was coming down from the sky.

Mando broke into a run, sprinting up the hill to protect Grogu. Before he reached the top, he saw the four black figures descending, retro-repulsors lowering them inside the circle of stones.

They were Moff Gideon's dark troopers.

There was nothing human about them—they weren't even alive. Soulless, red-eyed, unstoppable, they marched toward Grogu. One of the black-armored droids grabbed him from the stone, where the protective energy field had since dissipated, then ignited and shot skyward, rocketing back in the direction of the cruiser.

Mando reached instinctively behind him and realized he had no jet pack. He'd left it on the ground in the midst of the standoff with Fennec and Fett. A sudden sense of helplessness overwhelmed him, and he stood watching as the four dark troopers rose higher, out of sight.

There was a whoosh as Boba Fett's ship sliced across the sky behind them. Fennec picked up the comm, hailing Fett. "They've got the baby. Don't let them get away!"

"Affirmative," Fett's voice came back. "I have a lock."

Realizing what that meant, Mando turned to Fennec. "Stop him," he said. "I don't want the Child hurt."

Fennec keyed the comm again. "Abort pursuit. Disengage. Do not harm the Child."

"Copy," Fett replied. "I'll do a loose follow and see where they're headed."

Mando engaged his vision enhancement on the visor and observed the outline of Fett's ship rising higher into the expanse.

"They're back," Fett said. The words sounded hollow, disbelieving.

"Who?" Fennec asked.

"The Empire. They're back."

"That can't be," she said. "This area is under the jurisdiction of the New Republic."

"This isn't a spice dream," Fett replied through the comm. "I can see the Imperial cruiser with my own eyes. I'm heading down."

Mando stood motionless, still staring at the sky.

◆

Later Mando stood in the crater where his ship had been, sifting through ashes and debris. There wasn't much left to recover. Looking down, he saw a metal object and picked it up: the silver knob from the ship's controls. He gazed at it for a moment and slipped it into the pouch at his hip.

Then he saw something else—a long metal rod, seemingly unscathed in the explosion. Lifting it, he saw it was the beskar staff Ahsoka had given him. There wasn't a scratch on it. He glanced up, saw Fett and Fennec watching him, and raised the staff.

"This is all that survived," he said.

"Beskar?" Fett asked, and when Mando didn't answer, he beckoned the bounty hunter closer. "I want you to take a look at something." He activated a hologram on his bracer, displaying ray-traced sigils of identification. "My chain code has been encoded in this armor for twenty-five years." He pointed at the lineage tree. "You see? This is me. Boba Fett. This is my father, Jango Fett."

"Your father was a foundling," Mando said.

"Yes," Fett said. "He even fought in the Mandalorian Civil Wars."

"Then that armor belongs to you."

Fett nodded. "I appreciate its return."

"Then our deal is complete."

"Not quite," Fett said.

Mando glanced at him warily. "How so?"

"We agreed in exchange for the return of my armor we will ensure the safety of the Child."

The Mandalorian felt the weight of all his losses settling over him, heavier than the armor on his shoulders. "The Child's gone," he said.

"Until he is returned to you safely," Fett said, "we are in your debt." He turned to Fennec, who nodded her agreement, and Mando found himself looking over at Fett's ship.

He knew what he had to do.

CHAPTER 18

CARA DUNE HAD NOT expected to see the Mandalorian again so soon.

She was in her office in the city on Nevarro with her feet on her desk, finishing up the final reports of the day, when she glanced up and saw him standing there.

"I need your help," Mando said.

"Name it."

"I need you to locate someone in the prison registry."

Cara leaned forward, clicking on the display screen in front of her. "Let's see what we can do," she said.

"Ex-Imperial sharpshooter," Mando told her. "Last name Mayfeld. Apprehended near the Dilestri system on a derelict prison ship."

Cara typed, eyes scanning the data as it scrolled over her monitor. "Migs Mayfeld," she said. "Serving fifty years in Karthon Chop Fields for springing a prisoner himself. Accessory to the death of a New Republic offi-cer." She raised her gaze to Mando. "Sounds like a real piece of work. What do you want with him?"

Mando drew in a breath. "I need to spring him to help me locate Moff Gideon's light cruiser."

Cara frowned. "You know how I feel about the Empire." She pointed at her badge. "But these stripes mean there are rules I need to follow."

Mando met her gaze. There were a hundred things he could've said at that moment, but only one of them mattered.

"They have the kid," he said.

◆

Aboard the Imperial cruiser, Moff Gideon could already hear the sounds of crashing, accompanied by the dis-tant yelps and groans of the stormtroopers. He strode purposefully down the corridor and approached the cell door.

The hatch slid open, revealing chaos.

The Child sat on a bench, hands raised, flinging stormtroopers to and fro like puppets. The troopers scrambled to their feet and tried to back away, but they were no match for the power of the Force. With a single gesture, the Child threw them backward and smashed them into the walls, tossing them aside.

Gideon watched from the doorway. The smirk on his face was a mixture of pride and appreciation. This was exactly what he'd been hoping to find, and the Child had not disappointed him.

Two new troopers ran in behind him, blasters at the ready. "Set to stun," one of them said.

Gideon held up a finger. "Wait."

The beaten troopers collapsed, and the Child peered at them. He was breathing hard from the exertion. Gideon squatted down in front of him. "You've gotten very good with that," he said, seeing how the Child was struggling to remain conscious. "But it makes you oh so sleepy."

The Child's eyelids fluttered, scarcely able to stay open. Reaching down, Gideon drew out the Darksaber and switched it on. The Child's eyes opened again, transfixed by the shimmering black blade as it hovered overhead.

"Have you ever seen one of these before?" Gideon asked. "From years past?"

The Child brought up one hand as if to touch it, and Moff Gideon shook his head playfully. "Ah, ah, ah. You're not ready to play with such things." He switched off the blade. "Liable to put out an eye with one of these." Gazing at the Child's steadily sinking eyelids, he saw fatigue taking over again. "Looks like you could use a nice long sleep."

He nodded at the stormtrooper beside him, who raised his blaster and fired it, the ring of energy stunning the Child, and Grogu fell backward, eyes closed. Gideon's playful expression disappeared, replaced by a blank, dispassionate glare.

"Put it in shackles," he said, turning to the communications officer as he approached the door. "When we come out of hyperspace, send an encrypted message to Dr. Pershing. Let him know we have his donor."

"Yes, sir," the officer answered.

Gideon walked briskly down the corridor.

Behind him, the door sealed shut.

CHAPTER 19

THE DAYS MIGS MAYFELD spent on the rust-colored prison moon of Karthon had long ago become interchangeable. He awoke each morning with his ankle tethered to an electronic manacle and trudged out to the scrapyard, where he was forced to grapple with old tools and inoperable machines. Once he'd been an Imperial sharpshooter and then a rogue mercenary, but on Karthon he was just—

"Inmate Three-Four-Six-Six-Seven," said a mechanized voice behind him.

Perched up on the wing of the TIE fighter where he was struggling with a stubborn lug nut, Mayfeld didn't need to look down to know that the security droid was standing there, no doubt ready to accuse him of not working hard enough or fast enough. "What?"

"Inmate Three-Four-Six-Six-Seven," the droid repeated, "descend and receive new instructions."

Mayfeld slid down and landed next to the droid. "Can't you see I'm busy?"

"Inmate Three-Four-Six-Six-Seven, please salute Marshal Dune, ranger of the New Republic."

Mayfeld stared at the woman striding toward him as she showed her badge to the droid. Before he could ask for specifics, the shackle popped loose from his ankle. He kicked it off, baffled by this abrupt turn of events.

"I remand Prisoner Number Three-Four-Six-Six-Seven to my custody," the marshal said, sounding none too happy about it.

"Affirmative," the droid replied. "Inmate Three-Four-Six-Six-Seven, please follow Marshal Dune to transport."

Mayfeld didn't budge. "Is somebody going to tell me what's going on here?"

"Let's go," Cara said, already walking away. "I've got a job for you."

"Where are you taking me?" He looked at the droid. "Where is she taking me?"

The pronged weapon in the droid's hand began buzzing. "Inmate Three-Four-Six-Six-Seven, you have three seconds to comply with your new directive."

"Okay! All right," Mayfeld said, backing away and following the marshal through a maze of scrap and trash as they approached a ship that had landed in a cleared space. Mayfeld eyed the vessel suspiciously, its hatch open and ramp extended. "I mean, it's common courtesy to tell someone where it is you're taking 'em," he continued. "I don't think that's so hard to ask, do you? I mean—"

Then he saw the Mandalorian.

At least, he thought it was the Mandalorian. With a rush of relief, Mayfeld realized his mistake—this was someone else, wearing similar beskar armor and helmet, although this guy's gear appeared to be a different color. "Oh," he said with a laugh, "you know, for a second I thought you were this other guy. . . ."

Then he saw the Mandalorian.

And this time there could be no mistake, because Mayfeld had seen him in action up close.

Mando stood there. "Mayfeld," he said.

"Hey . . . Mando. Long time." Mayfeld tried to smile and quickly gave up. "So what, you came here to kill me?"

"All you need to know," Cara Dune said, "is that I bent a lot of rules to bring you along."

"Why am I so lucky?"

"Because you're Imperial."

"Hey," Mayfeld said, "that was a long time ago, all right?"

"But you still know your Imperial clearances and protocols," the Mandalorian said, "don't you?"

Mayfeld didn't bother to respond. If they'd come this far, they obviously already knew the answer.

As Boba Fett's starship rose from the surface of the moon, Mayfeld observed the rust-covered landscape shrinking away beneath him.

The Mandalorian wasted no time telling him what was expected. "We need coordinates for Moff Gideon's cruiser."

"Moff Gideon?" Mayfeld snorted. "Yeah, forget it. Just take me back to the scrapyard. I'm not doing that."

"They have his kid," Cara Dune said.

Mayfeld looked at Mando, thinking of the strange, wrinkly creature that had been traveling with the Mandalorian. "The little green guy?"

"Yeah," Cara said, "the little green guy."

"So, I help you guys get him back, you guys let me go?"

"That's not how this works," Cara said.

"Well, then what's in it for me?"

Cara's eyes were cold. "You get a better view."

Mayfeld sighed. "All right, but here's the thing, I can't get those coordinates unless I have access to an internal Imperial terminal." He thought for a second, trying to recall the name of the planet. "I believe there's one on Morak."

"Morak?" Mando repeated. "There's nothing on Morak."

"It's a secret Imperial mining hub, okay?" Mayfeld said. "If you can get me in there, I can get you the coordinates."

Mando leaned forward toward the cockpit. "Fett, punch in the coordinates to Morak."

"Copy that," Fett said, and prepared to jump to hyperspace.

◆

Some time later, they approached the planet where the mining colony was located. Mando, Fennec, Cara, and Mayfeld were sitting in the cargo area when Fett appeared from the cockpit.

"I did an initial scan of the planet," he said. Tapping a button on the display console, he brought up a holographic projection of the surface, indicating an outpost blinking red. "This is what you're talking about, right?"

"Yeah," Mayfeld said with a nod. "That's the refinery right there."

"Wonder what they're refining in there," Fennec said.

Fett checked the scan. "Looks like rhydonium," he said. "Highly volatile and explosive."

"Kinda like this one here, huh?" Mayfeld said, nodding at Cara, who ignored him.

"They have anti-aircraft cannons protecting it," Fett said.

Fennec studied the image. "And a platoon of security forces."

"So we go in quiet," Mando said. "Let's go get a closer look."

CHAPTER 20

THE SURFACE of the planet was wooded and largely undeveloped, with the exception of wide roads carved across the valley below to allow for the passage of massive, multi-wheeled Juggernaut transports that ran in and out of the mining tunnels. From their vantage point on the ridgeline above, the group surveyed the area. Fett's ship was partially hidden in the vegetation behind them.

"I'm not gonna need long inside," Mayfeld said. "So once I get the coordinates, you guys gotta get me out of there."

"You get to the roof," Fett said. "I'll drop in and pull you out."

"All right," Cara said. "Mayfeld and I will swap out for the drivers in the tunnel."

Mayfeld shook his head. "As much as I'd like to take

a road trip with rebel dropper here," he said, "that's not gonna work."

"Oh, yeah?" Cara said. "Why's that?"

"Because these remnant bases are set up and run by ex-ISB," Mayfeld informed her. "If you get scanned and your genetic signature shows up on any New Republic register you're gonna be detected, and it's guns out."

Cara glared at him. "You sure do know a lot about Imperial remnants."

"Hey, if you want to accuse me of something," Mayfeld snapped, "then just say it."

"We don't have time for this," Mando said. "Fennec will go."

"I'm wanted by the ISB," Fennec said. "I'll trip the alarm, too."

Mando looked at Fett, who shook his head. "Let's just say they might recognize my face," the old man growled.

"Great," Mayfeld said, "so I'm going in alone."

"No way," Cara said. "The minute he gets inside, he'll tip them off. He'll be a hero."

"Hey," Mayfeld said, "this wasn't my idea. I'm doing you guys a favor."

But Cara wasn't buying it. "Deal's off," she said. "I'm taking him back."

"I'll go," Mando said.

Mayfeld stared at him, incredulous. "Hey, buddy, I might be good at fast-talking, but I don't think I can explain away a guy in a Mando suit to Imperial guards. So unless you're gonna take off that helmet, it's gonna be me going in alone. Or else say goodbye to your little green friend."

Mando gazed down at the approaching Juggernaut, using the scanner in his visor to study the two helmeted drivers inside.

"You're not going alone," he said. "I'm coming with you. But I won't be showing my face."

At first it all went smoothly. Cara, Mayfeld, and Mando dropped onto the roof of the Juggernaut as it headed into the tunnel. It wasn't a quiet landing, but neither of the helmeted pilots inside the transport heard Cara Dune coming until it was too late. She surprised both of them with a lightning-quick series of blows and finished them off by simultaneously slamming both their heads against the control console, dropping them unconscious to the floor.

Moments later, the transport sat parked inside the tunnel. Cara stood watch while Mayfeld struggled into the uniform of one of the drivers. "This guy reeked," he complained. "Gloves are still wet. . . ."

From down the tunnel, Mando emerged, dressed in full combat driver armor and helmet. "Look at this," Mayfeld said. "Oh, the shame. Now that right there is worth the price of admission."

Cara raised an eyebrow at Mando. "Wish I could say it looked good on you," she said, "but I'd be lying."

"Just make sure you take out the rooftop gunners," Mando said, "or we're never getting out of here."

She nodded. "We got you."

"And take care of this." Mando handed her his armor and helmet in a bundle. It was not easy entrusting it to anyone, even a friend like Cara. "Keep it safe."

"I will," she assured him.

"Hey, guys?" Mayfeld said. "Still on the clock." He glanced at Mando. "What would they say on Mandalore?" Then he turned to Cara. "You know, it's a shame you're not coming with us. You got such a sunny disposition. Can't imagine how much fun you are in one of these."

Cara ignored him again, and Mayfeld and Mando headed for the Juggernaut.

It was time to roll.

CHAPTER 21

ONCE INSIDE the cockpit of the Juggernaut with the control panel in front of him, Mayfeld was a new man. He cracked his knuckles and tapped a switch, familiarizing himself with the controls, enjoying the freedom of the moment. "Arc coil, motivator . . . Ah, there we go. And we are off!"

He hit the accelerator, and the transport leapt forward, rolling down a road carved through dense jungle. After a moment, he glanced over at Mando. "Hey, how does it feel, huh?"

Mando said nothing, keeping his attention focused straight ahead.

"Hey, come on, man," Mayfeld said. "You still get to wear a helmet, right?" He paused. "All right, you know what, I'm taking this thing off. I can't see anything." He turned to Mando again after he'd removed his helmet.

"I don't know how you people wear those things. And by 'you people,' I do mean Mandalorians."

Mando didn't reply. They kept going, passing the wreckage of another Juggernaut. This one had been blown to smithereens, reduced to a twisted pile of scrap metal. Mayfeld was still frowning at it when chatter came through the comm. "Juggernaut Four, you're running a bit hot. Be sure and watch your heat limits."

"Copy that, Three," replied the driver. "We hit a couple bumps. Thanks for the heads-up."

Mayfeld squirmed a little in his seat, and Mando must've noticed his nerves. "Don't worry about the rhydonium," he said. "As long as you drive steady, you'll get us to the refinery."

The road went on, and the vehicle approached a group of small houses and huts with local villagers walking along the side of the road. Mando looked out at a group of children, and one of the kids made direct eye contact, gazing coldly back at him as the transport went by. Mayfeld chuckled.

"Empire, New Republic," he said. "It's all the same to these people. Invaders on their land is all we are." He drove on, warming to his idea. "I'm just saying, somewhere, someone in the galaxy is ruling and others are being ruled." He glanced at Mando. "I mean, look at your race. Do you really think all those people that died in wars fought by Mandalorians actually had a choice?"

Mando said nothing.

"So," Mayfeld continued, "how are they any different than the Empire? Look, if you were born on Mandalore, you believe one thing, if you're born on Alderaan, you believe something else." He tapped Mando on the shoulder to emphasize his point. "But guess what? Neither of them even exist anymore."

Mando turned to look away.

"Hey," Mayfeld said, "I'm just a realist. I'm a survivor. Just like you."

That was enough for Mando. "Let's get one thing straight," he said. "You and I are nothing alike."

"I dunno," Mayfeld went on, seemingly unfazed. "Seems to me like your rules start to change when you get desperate. I mean, look at you. You said you couldn't take your helmet off, and now you got a stormtrooper one on. So what's the rule?" He appeared genuinely curious. "Is it that you can't take off your Mando helmet, or you can't show your face? 'Cause there's a difference."

Silence from Mando.

"Look," Mayfeld continued, "I'm just saying, we're all the same. Everybody's got their lines they don't cross until things get messy. Far as I'm concerned, if you can make it through your day and still sleep at night, you're doing better than most."

"Control, this is Juggernaut Three," the driver's voice broke through the comm again. "We might be coming up on some route interference." The driver's voice rose in pitch, becoming panicked. "Control, Control, we need a new—" It broke off in a scream.

"What was that?" Mayfeld asked.

Up ahead, a massive fireball erupted along the tree line. A moment later, the operator's voice spoke calmly from the comm. "Juggernaut Three has been destroyed."

"Destroyed?" Mayfeld said.

Mando checked the onboard sensors, all of them still safely in the green. "The rhydonium is still stable," he said.

"Juggernaut Five," the operator continued, "maintain speed and course. Proceed with caution."

"Proceed with caution? Is she serious?"

KABOOM! Another explosion rang out in the distance, accompanied by another boiling cloud of flame in the sky. Mando checked the monitors showing the outside of the transport and realized this wasn't an accident.

They were under attack. From there Mando could see a motley band of Shydopp pirates riding atop a hovering skiff, preparing to board them as the skiff pulled even with the Juggernaut. The pirates had greenish-gray skin, giving them a faintly reptilian appearance, and their outfits—a mismatched wardrobe of vests, belts, and tunics—fluttered in the wind as they drew nearer. One of the pirates leapt off and grabbed hold of the side of the transport with a thud.

"What was that?" Mayfeld demanded. Mando powered down the window and looked back.

"Pirates," Mando said. "Keep driving. I'll take care of it." He leaned out. The pirate clinging to the side of the Juggernaut yanked a thermal detonator from his belt and activated it. Mando pulled his blaster and fired, missing the pirate as he clambered to the roof of the vehicle.

"Are you seriously shooting a blaster near rhydonium?" Mayfeld shouted.

"They have thermal detonators!" Mando said.

"Terrific."

"Just keep it steady," Mando told him. Climbing up through the hatch in the roof, he took aim at the nearest Shydopp raider, who was already in the process of reaching for the rhydonium cylinders, and shot him. With a whoop, the pirate rag-dolled backward off the rear of the Juggernaut, and Mando fired again, hitting the skiff, then watched it detonate in the road behind them.

"They're trying to blow the rhydonium," he called down.

"You think?" Mayfeld snapped. He was staring at the sensors on the dashboard, the volatility readout rising perilously with the jostling of the explosion. Up above, Mando was about to close the hatch when he saw two more skiffs careening up behind them, the Shydopps aboard howling and brandishing staffs and melee weapons.

"You should've left me in prison!" Mayfeld said.

Four pirates leapt onto the back of the transport. Mando raised his blaster and shot one of them, then pulled the trigger again. *Click*. Jammed. Glancing at the useless Imperial weapon, he tossed it at the pirates, who were charging him. Mando smashed one of the pirates in the face, snatched his spear, and swung it at the other Shydopp, knocking him over the edge. As the last of the pirates scampered toward him, Mando flung the spear and sent him flying off the Juggernaut.

But the second skiff was already closing in. "Mayfeld, pick it up!" Mando yelled down into the cockpit. "*Drive faster!*"

Behind the controls, Mayfeld jammed the accelerator

and the vehicle surged forward, rattling and bouncing hard on the dirt road. Almost immediately the rhydonium sensors began to jump and turn red, seconds away from meltdown. "I don't think faster's a good idea!" he said, and hit the brakes.

"What are you doing?" Mando shouted. The skiff was close enough that a second wave of pirates had already jumped aboard, heavily armed and intent on finishing the job. Taking hold of a staff, Mando managed to fight off the first two raiders, but the third knocked him flat and pinned him down while the fourth pirate reopened the hatch containing the rhydonium and pulled out another detonator, clicking it to life.

Jerking himself upright, Mando slammed his head into the pirate holding him down and kicked him over the side. He leapt to his feet and ran over to where the thermal detonator had been planted, yanking it loose from the rhydonium and flinging it at the skiff immediately behind them. The detonator went off with a deafening roar, blowing the skiff to bits.

Down below, Mayfeld saw the bridge coming up fast. "Mando," he called up, "I gotta stop. I can't cross at this speed!"

Mando glanced back. Through the smoke of the explosion he saw another skiff surging into view as another gang of pirates already prepared to board. They all had something in their hands, and after a moment Mando realized what it was.

Every single one of them was holding a thermal detonator.

Outnumbered and unarmed, he squared his shoulders and raised his fists to confront the inevitable. At this point there was nothing else to do except go down swinging.

A sudden volley of blaster fire began shredding the ground around them, spewing up massive chunks of earth on either side of the road. Mando ducked and looked around at a pair of TIE fighters roaring overhead, shooting at the skiff and blasting it to pieces, sending pirates flying everywhere.

Inside the transport, Mayfeld hooted with delight. Up ahead, troopers were already spilling out of the tunnel, firing at the pirates and waving the Juggernaut forward onto the bridge. Mando climbed down through the hatch with a groan of exhaustion, looked out the window, and saw troopers saluting them as they passed.

"Never thought you'd be happy to see storm-troopers," Mayfeld muttered.

CHAPTER 22

INSIDE THE GRIMY COURTYARD
of the rhydonium refinery, the salutes and cheers continued. Workers and Imperial troopers surrounded the Juggernaut with cries of "You did it!" as Mando and Mayfeld climbed down from the cab.

"Okay," Mayfeld said, keeping his voice low, "all we gotta do is find a terminal. It's probably in the officers' mess." He led Mando through the mob, saluting the others and nodding his thanks as they went along.

The officers' mess was a large, mostly empty space off the main courtyard with just a few Imperial officers sitting inside, eating and drinking and enjoying the privileges afforded to them. Peering in, Mando saw the kiosk containing the security terminal.

"There it is," Mayfeld said.

"Good luck," Mando said.

Mayfeld took a step into the mess hall. A moment later he came back looking pale and shaken. "I can't go in there."

"Why not?" Mando asked.

"That's Valin Hess."

"Who?"

"Valin Hess," Mayfeld said. "I used to serve under him."

Mando looked at the officer sitting at the table, who seemed to have noticed that he was being watched. "Will he recognize you?"

"I don't know," Mayfeld said. "I was just a field operative, but I'm not taking that chance. It's over."

"Let's just do this quick," Mando said, "and we can get out of here."

Mayfeld shook his head. "I can't do it, okay? We have to abort. I'm sorry."

"No." Mando put up his hand and stopped him. "I can't. If we don't get those coordinates, I'll lose the kid forever. Give me the data stick."

Mayfeld gave him a disbelieving look. "It's not gonna work," he said, and leaned in, his voice dropping to an urgent whisper. "In order to access the network, the terminal has to scan your face." He shook his head. "Let's go."

"Give it to me," Mando said. He took the stick from Mayfeld's hand and made his way into the mess hall, trying to be as inconspicuous as possible but immediately aware of the officers' eyes on him as he approached the terminal. Sliding the stick into the port, he waited. A red scanner illuminated his helmet, and the screen went red.

"Error," a digitized voice said. "Facial scan incomplete. Ten seconds to system shutdown. Six . . . five . . . four . . ."

Mando reached up and removed his helmet.

His face was exposed to the terminal but no one else. As the scanner ran its lights across his face, the lock screen vanished, replaced by the words *ACCESS IS GRANTED.*

Mando began typing, bringing up the schematic for Moff Gideon's cruiser, followed by the galactic coordinates on a star map. The plan was working. Everything he needed to find Grogu was right here in front of him.

"Trooper!" someone barked from across the room.

Mando froze, then started typing again as if he hadn't heard.

"Trooper!" It was Hess, snapping like a man not used to repeating himself. "Pay attention when your superior addresses you."

Mando pulled the stick from the terminal and turned to look at Hess, who was standing directly in front of him, glaring.

"What's your designation?" he asked.

"Transport crew," Mando said.

Hess frowned. "What?"

"My designation is transport copilot."

"No, son," Hess said. "What's your TK number?"

"My TK number is . . ." Mando hesitated.

"This is my commanding officer, TK-Five-Nine-Three, sir," Mayfeld cut in, striding over to join them. "I'm Imperial Combat Assault Transport Lieutenant TK-One-Eleven, sir, and I'm afraid you're going to have to speak up to him a little bit since his vessel lost pressure in Taanab."

Hess raised his voice, enunciating every syllable. "What's your name, Officer?"

"We just call him Brown Eyes," Mayfeld said. "Isn't that right, Officer?" He was already leading Mando away, out of the mess hall. "Come on, let's go fill out those TPS reports so we can go recharge the power coils."

"You're not dismissed," Hess said behind them.

They stopped. Then slowly, Mayfeld and Mando turned to look back at him.

"You the tank troopers who delivered the shipment of rhydonium?" Hess asked.

"Yes, sir," Mayfeld said, and a moment later, Mando echoed him.

"Well," Hess said, "you two managed to be the only transport today to deliver their shipment." His narrow face erupted into a grin. "Come with me. Let's get a drink." Then, patting Mando on the shoulder, he added, "Brown Eyes."

Mando and Mayfeld exchanged glances and followed Hess to his private table, away from the others. Hess flicked a hand to beckon to a nearby officer, who proceeded to pour them all glasses of wine.

"So what shall we toast to, boys?" Hess asked, glass already raised. "I could blather on about 'to health' or 'to success,' but I'd like to do something a little less rote."

"How about a toast to Operation Cinder," Mayfeld said.

Hess nodded approvingly. "Now there's a man who knows his history."

"No," Mayfeld said, "I don't just know it. I *lived* it." He sat forward, his eyes locked on the officer's. "I was in Burnin Konn."

The smile slid from Hess's face. "Burnin Konn?" he echoed.

Mayfeld nodded.

"That was a hard day," Hess said. "I had to make many unpleasant decisions."

"Yes, you did," Mayfeld said. As he spoke, he could feel something lighting up inside him, some all-but-forgotten ember of indignation beginning to glow bright red. "An entire city gone in moments along with everybody in it. We lost our whole division that day." He shook his head, marveling. "Man, that was like five, ten thousand people."

"Yep," Hess said. He was smiling again. His teeth looked very white. "All heroes of the Empire."

"Yeah," Mayfeld said, "and all dead."

"Well, it's a small sacrifice for the greater good, son."

"Depends on who you ask, don't you think?" Mayfeld said. His voice sounded different, gaining an edge, and Hess heard it, too.

"Whatcha getting at, trooper?"

"All those people," Mayfeld said, "the ones who died—was it good for them? Their families? The guys I served with? Civilians, those poor mud scuffers, died defending their homes, fighting for freedom. Was it good for 'em?"

Hearing all this, Hess's grin was still hanging in there, sharper and more wolfish than ever. If anything, he seemed to be enjoying this conversation more than he'd expected. "But we've outlasted them, son. They're eating themselves alive. The New Republic is in complete disarray, and we grow stronger."

Listening, Mayfeld felt the burning coal in his chest starting to grow even hotter. On the opposite side of the table, Officer Hess, still caught up in his own rhetoric, scarcely seemed to notice, but Mando, looking back and forth between the two men, saw it building up.

"You see, with the rhydonium you've delivered," Hess continued, "we can create havoc that's gonna make Burnin Konn just pale by comparison. And then they're gonna turn to us once again. You see, boys"—he leaned in almost conspiratorially, as if to take Mayfeld and Mando into his confidence, to impart some profound wisdom—"everybody thinks they want freedom. But what they really want is order."

Mayfeld sat back and took in a deep breath. All at once he felt very calm, waiting while Hess finished his speech.

"And when they realize that," Hess said, "they're gonna welcome us back with open arms." He raised his glass and beamed at Mayfeld, his grin broader than ever. "To the Empire."

That was when Mayfeld shot him.

The noise of the shot inside the officers' mess was very loud.

Mayfeld lowered his weapon. Mando sat there staring at him. In the beat that followed, every officer in the hall turned to look at him. Mayfeld, the former Imperial sharpshooter, raised his blaster again with unerring precision and shot all of them where they stood. Mando grabbed Hess's sidearm and finished off the last one himself.

Mayfeld handed the Mandalorian his helmet. "You did what you had to do," he said, looking away. "I never saw your face."

Mando put the helmet on and nodded his thanks.

"Security to main commons," a voice on the overhead speaker rang out. "Security to main commons."

From outside, shoretroopers were already rushing in. Jumping up behind the table, Mando kicked the window loose, and he and Mayfeld stepped out onto the ledge.

On the ridge above the refinery, Fennec and Cara looked through rifle scopes as Mando and Mayfeld crept out along the exterior wall, hundreds of meters above the basin below. Troopers were already climbing out behind them.

"South wall," Fennec said, "halfway up."

"Got 'em," Cara said. She fired down on the trooper nearest Mando, sending him plummeting. Fennec fired alongside her, the two of them taking out the artillery troopers manning the cannons mounted to the rooftop of the refinery.

Fennec keyed her comlink, signaling Boba Fett. "We're on," she said. "Start your run."

"On my way," Fett answered.

By the time Mando and Mayfeld reached the rooftop, there was no time to hesitate. If Fennec and Cara hadn't taken out the rest of the gunners, it was too late to turn back. They ran hard, ducking gunfire from the remaining Imperials, and Mando glanced up to see Boba Fett's ship skimming down from overhead.

The hatchway was already open.

"Go!" Mayfeld was shouting. "Go, go, go!"

Leaping from the edge of the rooftop, Mando landed on the ramp and scrambled inside, followed by Mayfeld as the ship banked hard and began a sharp ascent. Mayfeld caught his breath and turned to look down at the refinery.

"Hand me that cycler rifle," he said.

Mando pulled the Tusken Raider rifle off the wall

and passed it to Mayfeld. He brought the weapon to his shoulder, sighting down on the Juggernaut still parked in the courtyard. Through the scope he could see very clearly the open hatch, and the rhydonium inside.

Drawing a bead on the rhydonium, Mayfeld took in a breath, let it out slowly, and pulled the trigger.

Direct hit.

FOOOM! For a moment the explosion seemed to suck everything into itself and then released a ground-shaking concussion that triggered a series of even bigger aftershocks as the entire base was obliterated.

Mayfeld watched it go. He turned to Mando, handing him the rifle.

"We all need to sleep at night," he said.

◆

Later, having landed away from what remained of the refinery, Mayfeld and Mando waited on the ramp of Fett's ship as Cara and Fennec emerged from the jungle.

"Well," Mayfeld said, "looks like it's back to the scrap heap."

Mando turned to him. "Thank you for helping."

"Yeah," Mayfeld said. "Good luck getting your kid back." He walked toward Cara, wrists extended for the cuffs of justice. "All right, Officer, take me back."

"That was some nice shooting back there," Cara said.

"Oh, you saw that?" Mayfeld actually seemed surprised. "Yeah, that wasn't part of the plan. Just getting some stuff off my chest."

Cara exchanged glances with Mando and Fennec. "You know," she said, "it's too bad Mayfeld didn't make it out alive back there."

"Yeah," Mando said. "Too bad."

Mayfeld stared at them, scowling. "What are you talking about?"

"Looked to me like Prisoner Three-Four-Six-Six-Seven died in the refinery explosion on Morak," Cara said.

A look of understanding began to creep over Mayfeld's face. "Does that mean I can go?" he asked. "Huh? 'Cause I will." Cara gave the slightest of shrugs. Mayfeld took a step away, then another, glancing back. "Okay," he said, and disappeared into the foliage, already gone.

Cara turned to Mando as they started up the ramp. "You get the coordinates on Moff Gideon?" she asked.

Mando nodded. "We did."

"What's our next move?"

He told her.

Aboard the Imperial light cruiser, the communications officer summoned Moff Gideon to the bridge. "Sir, you should see this."

Gideon paused, frowning, and pressed a button. The hologram that appeared in front of him showed the Mandalorian staring back at him, speaking words that Gideon recognized all too well.

"Moff Gideon," Mando said. "You have something I want. You may think you have some idea what you are in possession of, but you do not. Soon he will be back with me. He means more to me than you will ever know."

Gideon stood staring at the Mandalorian, motionless, silent.

The hologram disappeared.

CHAPTER 23

BOBA FETT'S SHIP WAS a customized *Firespray-31*-class patrol and attack craft equipped with a Class 1 hyperdrive and twin blaster cannons.

All of which meant it was extremely fast, and extremely deadly.

At the moment these features and others were on full display as it moved in on a helpless *Lambda*-class Imperial shuttle, firing as it closed the distance and overtook the smaller, slower vessel. The shuttle corkscrewed into evasive action, but it was no contest. The Firespray was already closing the distance like a bird of prey, firing its ion cannon.

All at once the shuttle went dead in space. Inside the cockpit, two pilots struggled to restore power to the system while the bearded, bespectacled man between them gaped in panic at this unexpected development.

"What's going on?" Dr. Pershing demanded. "Who are they?"

"I suggest you shut your mouth," the pilot told him. "This isn't your laboratory."

"They hit us with an ion cannon." The copilot surveyed the control panel, checking a half dozen instruments and finding them all unresponsive. "Avionics are down. Comms are down."

A voice broke through the speaker, deadly calm: "Lower your shields," Boba Fett said. "Disengage all transponders. Prepare for boarding."

Obeying instantly, the pilot activated the manual override, turning off the shields and retracting the shuttle's wings in preparation to receive whoever or whatever had disabled his ship.

"They're pirates," Dr. Pershing said. "Shouldn't we fight?"

"I don't have a death wish," the pilot said. "Do you?"

Pershing didn't get a chance to answer before a loud clang from above announced the arrival of the other ship. Moments later, the hatch behind them opened and the Mandalorian entered the cockpit. Pershing recognized him immediately, and all the color drained out of his face.

"Before you make a mistake," the pilot told Mando, "this is Dr. Pershing."

"We've met," Mando said, not taking his eyes off Pershing. "Is the kid alive?"

Pershing managed a frantic nod. "Yes, he's on the cruiser—"

The pilot drew his pistol and grabbed Pershing around the neck, jamming the blaster against the doctor's head. Mando didn't move. Behind him, Cara had stepped into the cockpit, watching the moment unfold. The pilot glared at her.

"Stay back, dropper."

"Easy, pal," the copilot said, keeping his voice reasonable. He looked at Mando and Cara. "Okay, I'm not with him. We can work something out—"

The pilot shot him. The pilot's eyes were huge and darting too quickly around the cockpit, as if searching for solutions that weren't presenting themselves fast enough.

"Drop your weapon," Cara said.

"No," the pilot said. "No, you listen to me. This is a top-tier target of the New Republic. This is a clone engineer. And if they find out he's dead because of you, you're gonna wish you never left Alderaan."

Cara's eyes narrowed, and her face grew tense.

"I saw the tear on your cheek," the pilot said. "You wanna know what else I saw?" He grinned. "I saw your planet destroyed. I was on the Death Star."

"Which one?" Cara asked. Her voice was acid.

"You think you're funny?" the pilot demanded. "Do you know how many millions were killed on those bases? As the galaxy cheered?"

"Drop your blaster," Cara said, her own weapon pointed at the pilot. "Last chance."

"Destroying your planet was a small price to pay to rid the galaxy of terrorism," he said.

Cara pulled the trigger, the blaster round grazing the doctor's ear before it slammed into the pilot, dropping him instantly to the ground. As the pilot's body fell still, Pershing held his singed face and began to scream.

Cara turned and walked off.

◆

Boba Fett's starship angled out of the sky and swooped into the docking row in the bustling spaceport of Lafete. The nearest building was an establishment whose main purpose seemed to be serving travelers and long-haul fliers along the major galactic trade routes. As they walked in, Mando recognized the Gauntlet that belonged to Bo-Katan.

He and Boba Fett stopped and gazed across the

darkened room where two figures sat at a table in the back. Bo-Katan and Koska had their helmets off, sipping flagons of the local brew.

Mando and Fett approached the table. The other customers fell silent, eyeing their armor with visible nervousness, and began rising from their seats. Little by little, the place emptied out.

Bo-Katan and Koska turned to look at them.

"I need your help," Mando said.

Bo gazed at the two of them, her expression cool. "Not all Mandalorians are bounty hunters," she said. "Some of us serve a higher purpose."

"They took the Child," Mando said.

"Who?"

"Moff Gideon."

Her face became grim. "You'll never find him."

"We don't need these two," Boba Fett said. "Let's get out of here."

Bo-Katan glared at Fett. "You are not a Mandalorian."

"Never said I was," Fett said.

"I didn't know sidekicks were allowed to talk," Koska chided him.

With a chuckle, Fett walked over to where she was sitting. "Well, if that isn't the Quacta calling the Stifling slimy."

Koska stood up, eyes locked on his visor.

"Easy there, little one," Fett said.

Koska was tensed up, ready to fight. "You'll be talking through the window of a bacta tank," she snarled.

"Easy," Bo-Katan said, stepping in between them. "Save it for the Imps."

"We have his coordinates," Mando told her.

With those words, everything about Bo-Katan's demeanor changed. She stared at him. "You can take me to Moff Gideon?"

"The Moff has a light cruiser," Mando said. "It could be helpful in your effort to regain Mandalore."

Boba Fett snorted. "You gotta be kidding me," he said. "Mandalore? The Empire turned that planet to glass."

"You're a disgrace to your armor!" Bo-Katan told him.

"This armor belonged to my father."

"Don't you mean your donor?" she said, edging closer. "You are a clone. I've heard your voice thousands of times."

"Mine might be the last you hear," Fett grunted.

That was enough for Koska. She leapt at him, fists flying. Grappling with her, Fett slammed her into a table, splitting it in half with the force of impact. Before she could regain her equilibrium, he fired a cable from his wrist, lassoing her. Koska grabbed the wire and pulled him toward her, then flipped him into another table. Both of them lunged up and forward at the same time, igniting their flamethrowers.

"Enough!" Bo-Katan shouted. "Both of you!" She shook her head as they stepped back from each other. "If we'd shown half that spine to the Empire, we would've never lost our planet." She turned to Mando. "We will help you. In exchange, we will keep that ship to retake Mandalore. If you should manage to finish your quest, I would have you reconsider joining our efforts. Mandalorians have been in exile from our homeworld for far too long."

"Fair enough," Mando said as they started to go.

"One more thing."

"Yes?"

"Gideon has a weapon that once belonged to me," Bo-Katan said. "It is an ancient weapon. It can cut through anything."

"Almost anything," Koska amended.

"It cannot cut through pure beskar," Bo-Katan said. "I will kill the Moff and retake what is rightfully mine." She spoke with the confidence of one who had already glimpsed her destiny and was determined to take it. "With the Darksaber restored to me, Mandalore will finally be within reach."

"Help me rescue the Child," Mando told her, "and you can have whatever you want. He is my only priority."

Aboard Fett's ship, the group conferred to plan their next move. Dr. Pershing sat off to the side, handcuffed, listening as Bo-Katan pointed to the holographic schematics of their target.

"This is Moff Gideon's Imperial light cruiser," she said. "In the old days it would carry a crew of several hundred. Now it operates with a tiny fraction of that."

"Your assessment is misleading," Pershing said.

Cara rolled her eyes. "Oh, great, an objective opinion."

"This isn't subterfuge," Pershing said. "I assure you." He turned to face the group. "There is a garrison of dark troopers on board. They're the ones who abducted the Child."

"How many troopers do they have in those suits?" Mando asked.

"These are third-generation design," Pershing said. "They are no longer suits. The human inside was the final weakness to be solved. They're droids."

"Where are they bivouacked?" Fennec asked.

Indicating the hologram, Pershing gestured to a

cargo hold on the periphery of the cruiser. "They are held in cold storage in the cargo bay. They draw too much power to be kept at ready."

"How long to power up?" Fennec asked.

"A few minutes, perhaps," Pershing said.

Mando looked at him. "Where is the Child being held?"

Pershing pointed with his handcuffed hands to a chamber at the center of a hallway on the hologram. "This is the brig. He is being held here under armed guard."

"Very well," Bo-Katan said. "We split into two parties."

Mando shook his head. "I go alone."

"Fine." Bo-Katan nodded at the diagram of the ship, illustrating her plan as she described it. "Phase one: Lambda shuttle issues a distress call. Two: we come in hot and emergency land at the mouth of the fighter launch tube, cutting off any potential interceptors. Koska, Fennec, Dune, and myself disembark with maximum initiative." She paused. "Once we've neutralized the launch bay, we move through these tandem decks in a penetration maneuver."

"And me?" Mando asked.

"We'll be misdirection," Bo-Katan said. "Once we draw a crowd, you slip through the shadows, get the kid."

"Those dark troopers," Cara said, "they're gonna be a real skank in the scud pie."

"Their bay is on your way to the brig," Bo told Mando. She turned to Pershing. "Can he make it there before they deploy?"

Pershing thought about it. "It's possible."

"Here." Fennec pulled Pershing's cylinder from his pocket and gave it to Mando. "Take his code cylinder and seal off their holding bay. Anyone else, we can handle."

Mando nodded. He saw it now, how it would go and what he needed to do. Everything depended on every part of the plan working.

"We'll meet at the bridge," he said.

CHAPTER 24

THE FIRESPRAY BARRELED through hyperspace with the Lambda alongside it, both ships locked on to the coordinates of the Moff's cruiser. Inside the shuttle, Cara turned to address the group. "As soon as we land," she said, "we head for the bridge."

"Moff Gideon is mine," Bo-Katan said. "Got it?"

"He's ex-ISB," Cara said. "He's got a lot of information. I need him alive."

Bo glanced at her. "I don't care what happens to him as long as he surrenders to *me*."

Fett's voice came through the comm. "Prepare to exit jump space."

"Copy that," Bo-Katan told him. "Get the hell out of there as soon as they clear us to dock. And your shots have to look convincing."

"Power on those shields, princess," Fett retorted. "I'll put on a good show."

"Watch out for those deck cannons," Bo-Katan reminded him.

"Don't worry about me," Fett said. "Just be careful in there."

There was nothing more to say. Everyone knew their roles. Koska checked the controls. "Exiting hyperspace in three . . . two . . . one . . ."

They popped out of hyperspace and into battle.

◆

"This is Lambda shuttle two-seven-four-three," came a panicked voice from the comm. "Requesting immediate emergency docking! *We are under attack!*"

Moff Gideon stood on the bridge of the cruiser, gazing over the shoulder of the bridge officer. He didn't speak, simply listened.

Ever since receiving the hologram from the Mandalorian, his instincts had been on high alert as he focused on the plan of action. When Pershing arrived, they would extract what they needed from the Child and bring glory to the Empire once more.

◆

"Repeat, requesting emergency docking," Bo-Katan said into the comm. She brought the shuttle screaming into the cruiser's airspace with Fett's ship hot on its tail, deftly missing the shuttle with its cannon fire to complete this pageant of catastrophe. Some of Fett's shots were close enough to almost graze the ship.

"Copy, Lambda shuttle," the communications officer answered. "Request received. . . ." There was a slight delay, and then the voice continued. "Stay clear of the launch tube. Deploying fighter squadron—"

Bo gripped the throttle and brought the shuttle in tight, racing straight for the Imperial ship. From there, she could already see the tube opening, and watched as a pair of TIE fighters shifted onto the launch track. At this speed and trajectory, the fighters would have to swerve out of her way to avoid getting hit, but she couldn't turn back.

"Request denied!" the comms officer shouted. "Clear the launch tube until fighters deploy!"

"Negative!" Bo-Katan snapped back. "We are under attack!" The TIEs that had just flown out of the tube peeled off in either direction a split second before she would've collided with them, and the shuttle plowed headlong through the opening, retracting its wings as it smashed and clattered along the concourse and hit the deck, metal scraping and squealing as the shuttle slid down the length of the tube and finally ground to a halt.

Deck officers and stormtroopers fanned out around them, rushing toward the stalled shuttle, gesturing furiously as they approached. The ramp of the shuttle had already begun to lower as Bo, Cara, Fennec, and Koska ran down.

"What are you doing?" one of the officers yelled. "Clear the area! Get this thing—"

The shooting started almost immediately. Fennec's sniper rifle was already out and squeezing off shots while Cara stood beside her laying down automatic fire. The two Mandalorian warriors ignited their jet packs, blazing to the doors. Landing, they took out the remaining deck crew before most of the Imperials could manage to shoot back.

As the smoke lifted, Mando emerged down the ramp.

He was alone, the others having already cleared the tube on their way to the bridge. He had his blaster in hand, and the beskar staff was slung across his back in place of his jet pack. Stepping over the bodies of stormtroopers and deck officers, he made his way quickly into the shadows.

Grogu was in there somewhere.

And the clock was ticking.

"All clear," Koska said.

"A little too clear." Bo-Katan was scanning the perimeter, blaster out and pointed ahead of them. "Keep your eyes open."

They were passing through some sort of cargo holding area, its dimly lit recesses creepily quiet. The only sounds were the faint whirr of climate-control systems and beneath it, the steady pulsating hum of the ship's massive engines. Up ahead, Cara and Fennec slipped through the maze of crates and shipping pallets, all their senses alert to any sign of activity.

A stormtrooper popped into view and Cara shot him. Two more troopers followed him, returning fire. "Freeze!" one of them ordered. "Don't move! Drop the blaster!"

Fennec and Cara exchanged knowing glances.

Instead of dropping their weapons, they dropped the troopers.

But more Imperials were already spilling out to take their place. If they were going to make it to the bridge, they were going to have to shoot their way out.

Suddenly Koska and Bo-Katan jetted alongside them, flamethrowers roaring toward the next wave of troopers. Cara squeezed off another round, and the blaster fell silent in her hand.

"My gun's jammed!" she shouted.

"I got you," Fennec said, taking out the stormtrooper who had been about to shoot her, and they edged forward, Cara using the rifle as a bludgeon to smash the next trooper unlucky enough to be in her way. Fennec took out the next with her rifle, and Cara gave her a quick, appreciative nod.

"Thanks."

The two Mandalorian warriors had already taken point, moving through the end of the holding bay toward the dark tunnels beyond it. Stepping into a waiting elevator, Koska and Bo took a deep, collective breath to prepare for what was next while Cara struggled to clear her blaster.

"*Dank farrik!*" Cara snapped, wrestling with the weapon. "Son of a mud scuffer!"

Bo glanced at her. "Are you sure you don't need any help?"

Cara slammed the butt of the rifle against the floor of the elevator and felt it come back to life in her grasp. "I think that did it," she said. "Excuse me."

The doors opened, and they started shooting.

Reaching the dark trooper bay, Mando realized it was too late. Moff Gideon had already powered up his army of red-eyed droids. He could see them marching in lockstep, deadly and unstoppable.

Jamming the code cylinder into the panel, he activated the bay's containment systems and sealed the door. The hatch was almost shut when a pair of black hands squeezed through and forced the doors back open. Glaring out at him with red, unblinking eyes, the dark trooper grabbed Mando by the throat, swung him forward, and slammed him to the floor.

Mando felt all the breath being knocked out of him. He raised his arm and released a geyser of flame, followed by the whistling birds, exhausting all the weapons in his arsenal, but the dark trooper kept coming. It grabbed him, smashed him against the wall, and began pounding its fist into his helmet with a steady unstoppable series of blows until it had pushed Mando's helmet through the panel behind him, rupturing a gas main.

Mando took hold of the beskar staff, thrust it forward, and rammed it into the point where the droid's helmet was attached to its body. A sudden swarm of sparks spewed out from underneath the helmet. With all his strength, Mando jerked the rod down hard to wrench the thing's head off completely and sent the decapitated droid staggering backward, abruptly confused and malfunctioning into total collapse.

Mando ran back over to the panel by the door where the other dark troopers were pounding against the transparisteel. It was already beginning to crack and strain against the force of their attack. Mando hit a switch, opening the doors on the other side of the bay.

With a whoosh, the entire chamber depressurized, blowing the dark troopers out into space.

Within seconds, Fennec, Cara, and the two Mandalorian warriors reached the bridge. The bridge crew and remaining troopers fired from behind their control consoles, but they were no match for the foursome. For the first time they were fighting together as a team, each knowing her role without question or hesitation, rather than fighting as individuals.

Koska ran to the controls and hit a series of buttons. "Weapons system is disarmed," she reported.

Bo-Katan looked around with a sense of increasing unease and asked the question that was on all their minds.

"Where's Gideon?"

Two stormtroopers stood guard outside the sealed prison cell. When they saw Mando coming, they opened fire, but not fast enough.

With lightning speed, Mando brandished the beskar rod, clubbing one of the troopers across the helmet and knocking him out. He brought the bar around to press it against the throat of the second trooper, yanking tight until the Imperial stopped kicking and his body fell slack. Mando dropped him, then turned and slipped the key cylinder into the locked hatchway. The cell doors opened with a soft whoosh. Blaster in hand, he stepped forward.

Grogu was sitting there.

The child looked frightened and confused. A pair of manacles glowed around his tiny wrists.

Standing above him, Moff Gideon held the Darksaber over Grogu's head.

Gideon stared at Mando, motionless. "Drop the blaster," Gideon said. "Slowly."

Mando put it down.

"Now, kick it over to me," the Moff said.

Mando did as he was told.

"Very nice," Gideon said.

"Give me the kid," Mando said.

Gideon didn't move. "The kid is just fine where is." He gestured with the saber, moving it back and forth through the air above Grogu's wrinkled head as if transfixed by the weapon's power. "Mesmerizing, isn't it? Used to belong to Bo-Katan." He returned his gaze to Mando. "Yes, I know you're traveling with Bo-Katan. A friendly piece of advice: assume that I know everything. Like the fact that your wrist launcher has fired its one and only salvo."

"Where is this going?" Mando asked.

"This is where it's going." The Moff's voice hardened, shedding all pretense of civility. "I'm guessing that Bo-Katan and her boarding party have arrived at the bridge seeking me or, more accurately, *this*." He gestured again with the Darksaber. "But I'm not there. And I imagine that they've killed everyone on the bridge, being the murderous savages they are, and now they're beginning to panic." He glanced at Mando curiously. "Do you know why? Because it brings power. Whoever wields this sword has the right to lay claim to the Mandalorian throne."

"You keep it," Mando said. "I just want the kid."

Moff Gideon paused for a moment, as if weighing his options. "Very well," he said. "I've already gotten what I need from him. His blood." His tone had changed again, becoming reasonable, as if he and the Mandalorian were old acquaintances discussing matters they could both readily agree on. "All I wanted was to study his blood. This child is extremely gifted and has been blessed with rare properties that have the potential to bring order back to the galaxy."

Mando waited without response. Gideon studied the Child, observing the way Grogu was looking at his protector.

"I see your bond with him," the Moff said. "Take him. But you will leave my ship immediately, and we will go our separate ways."

Mando bent down. As he reached for Grogu, Moff Gideon lunged, striking with the Darksaber. There was a sudden crash as the blade met beskar. Mando parried with his forearm bracer and drew the spear slung over his shoulder with one fluid motion. Using the rod, he blocked the saber, but Gideon was already counter-attacking, coming at him with a flurry of vicious thrusts and slashes as they moved across the cell and outward into the adjoining corridor.

The Moff came at him again, and this time Mando barely got the spear up fast enough. Moving down the hall, Gideon kept coming, the edge of the Darksaber dragging along the wall, throwing off showers of sparks and gouging a deep hole in the ship as he drew closer. Mando kicked him backward, fired his grappling hook, and snared Gideon, but the Moff slashed through it easily and charged ahead with a snarl.

Mando flicked the spear forward, twisting, and knocked the sword from Gideon's hand. It skidded down the hallway, sparking into the wall. Whipping the spear around, Mando slammed his opponent across the head, toppling him, then spun the rod around so the sharp end was angled straight down at Gideon's throat.

Gideon peered up at him, smiling.

"You're sparing my life," he said. "Well, this should be interesting."

CHAPTER 25

ON THE BRIDGE, Cara and Fennec were waiting with Bo-Katan and Koska when the door opened. The Mandalorians had already removed their helmets, and when Bo-Katan saw who it was, she snapped her wrist blade out and prepared to fight. Then, slowly, she lowered it, a scowl of confusion forming on her brow.

Mando tossed Moff Gideon onto the bridge. Gideon was wearing the manacles, and Mando walked past him, carrying the Child in one hand and the Darksaber in the other.

Bo's frown deepened. "What happened?"

"He brought him in alive, that's what happened," Cara said. "And now the New Republic's gonna have to double the payment."

Moff Gideon shook his head. "That's not what she's talking about," he said with a slight smile, gazing up

Bo-Katan. "Why don't you kill him now and take it?" Then, looking back at Mando, his smile broadened. "It's yours now."

"What is?" Mando asked.

"The Darksaber. It belongs to you."

Mando deactivated the saber and extended it to Bo-Katan. "Now it belongs to her."

But Bo-Katan didn't reach for it. Instead she stood motionless, arms at her sides, not responding. On the floor between them, Moff Gideon spoke again, sounding delighted. "She can't take it," he told Mando. "It must be won in battle. In order for her to wield the Darksaber again, she would need to defeat you in combat."

"I yield," Mando said, the saber still outstretched in front of him. "It's yours."

Moff Gideon chuckled, enjoying himself thoroughly. "Oh, no," he said. "It doesn't work that way. The Darksaber doesn't have power. The story does. Without that blade, she's a pretender to the throne."

Mando waited for Bo-Katan to argue. She didn't.

"He's right," she said.

"me on," Mando said. "Just take it."

'g moment nobody moved. Then from the
'em, the ship's proximity alarm started

going off. Moff Gideon raised an eyebrow. "Well, per-haps she'll get another crack at it," he said.

Fennec was watching the monitor at the scanner station. "The ray shields have been breached," she said. "We're being boarded."

"How many life-forms?" Bo asked.

Fennec looked up in surprise. "None."

Gideon rose to his feet. "You are about to face off with the dark troopers," he said, gazing at Mando. "You had your hands full with one. Let's see how you do against a platoon."

Bo checked the surveillance monitors, which showed rows of the dark troopers marching down the corridor, weapons raised and ready. They moved throughout the ship, as formidable and inevitable as death itself. Soon Bo-Katan and the others could hear the sound of the boots outside, echoing through the vessel.

"They're headed this way," she said.

Grogu stirred uneasily in Mando's arms. He set the Child down in a safe spot. "Don't worry, kid. I'm gonna get you out of here."

"Seal the blast doors," Fennec said.

The door slammed down as Koska hit the button.

An instant later, Koska turned from the viewing screen to alert the others. Outside the doors, the marching sound had stopped.

"They're here," she said.

A hush fell across the bridge. Fennec picked up her rifle, and Cara raised her blaster, sighting down the barrel. Koska and Bo-Katan put their helmets on and drew their weapons, preparing for what would happen next.

Outside, the dark troopers began hammering their fists against the blast doors. Steadily, unceasingly. Already, the doors were starting to shake and shift from the impact.

Gideon looked up at Mando. "You have an impressive fire team protecting you," he said. "But I think we all know that after a valiant stand, everyone in this room will be dead but me and the Child."

Mando didn't reply. The pounding continued. The doors were starting to deform from the accelerated barrage, the gap splitting open, widening with every blow. It wouldn't be long.

Mando switched the saber to his left hand and drew his blaster with his right. The others stepped forward around him, preparing for the breach.

On the console, the alarm went off again.

Mando turned and looked around as a ship streaked by outside. The others were staring at it, too.

"An X-wing," Koska said.

"One X-wing?" Cara said. "Great. We're saved."

Bo-Katan keyed the comm. "Incoming craft, identify yourself."

No answer. On the monitor screen, they watched as the X-wing glided into the docking tube, preparing for landing. On the floor where Mando had placed him, Grogu sat up, ears twitching, eyes widening.

Then, outside the blast doors, the pounding stopped.

Fennec and Cara glanced at each other. The bridge was suddenly, unnervingly quiet.

For the first time, a look of uncertainty spread over Moff Gideon's face.

"Why did they stop?" Fennec asked.

The group lowered their weapons, watching the monitors. On-screen, a cloaked figure moved down the corridor, wielding a glowing green lightsaber. The ship's security cameras could barely resolve the bright image of the weapon as it swept by.

The dark troopers moved to attack, but the figure disarmed them quickly, deflecting the blaster shots with ease. The figure moved forward and sliced through the droids, their bodies falling in pieces to the floor as the figure drew nearer.

"A Jedi," Bo-Katan whispered.

Moff Gideon's eyes had grown with terror and realization. He lunged at Bo-Katan and grabbed her blaster with his cuffed hands, firing at her repeatedly. The blaster shots ricocheted off her armor, but one of them cut between the beskar plates, and she screamed and fell to the ground, clutching her leg.

Whirling, Gideon aimed the blaster at Grogu. Mando leapt forward, throwing himself in front of the Child, taking the hit across his breastplate. Koska, Fennec, and Bo all trained their weapons on Gideon.

"Drop it!" Fennec shouted.

Seeing there was no choice, Gideon swung the blaster up underneath his own chin. Before he could pull the trigger, Cara stepped in and drove her elbow into his face, dropping him. Gideon slumped to the floor, unconscious.

Mando glanced over at the Child, who had approached the monitor screen and pressed his hand against it, watching with rapt attention as the cloaked figure made their way to the elevator leading to the bridge. The figure stepped inside, and the elevator began to rise.

Up above, on the other side of the blast doors, the dark troopers had turned toward the elevator, waiting.

The doors opened.

The troopers attacked.

◆

What happened next couldn't really be called a fight. The cloaked figure swung the lightsaber through the army of Imperial droids, cutting a path of seared metal and sparks, moving through their ranks unscathed and leaving nothing but smoke and wreckage behind. More dark troopers plowed forward, and the figure dismissed them with a wave of the hand, flinging them aside with an authority that had nothing to do with firepower. As the last of the droids lunged, the figure raised one hand and froze the thing where it stood, crushing it from within, demolishing it with a gesture.

The figure stopped before the blast doors.

On the bridge, Mando looked at the Child, watching the monitors. Grogu turned and focused his attention on the doors, and Mando reached down and scooped him up.

"Open the doors." Walking over to where Fennec stood by the controls, he looked at her. "I said, open the doors."

"Are you crazy?" Fennec asked.

Mando set the Child down and hit the switch. The blast doors opened, and the figure stepped inside, the blade of the lightsaber glowing green through the smoke. Mando and the others stared at the figure as they approached, switched off the weapon, and lowered their hood.

The Jedi known as Luke Skywalker gazed at the group. Grogu peered at him, eyes wide.

"Are you a Jedi?" Mando asked.

Luke nodded. "I am." He reached out to Grogu. "Come, little one."

The Child looked up at Mando, murmuring uncertainly.

"He doesn't want to go with you," Mando said.

"He wants your permission," Luke said. "He is strong with the Force, but talent without training is nothing." He looked at Mando. "I will give my life to protect the Child, but he will not be safe until he masters his abilities."

Grogu was still staring at Mando. Reaching down, Mando scooped him up again. "Go on," he said. "That's who you belong with. He's one of your kind. I'll see you again, I promise."

The Child reached out to Mando's helmet. After a moment, Mando slowly removed it, allowing the Child to see his face for the first time. Grogu's eyes brightened at the man gazing back at him, and he touched his hand to Mando's face.

"All right, pal," Mando said. "It's time to go. Don't be afraid." He squatted down and set the Child on the floor, waiting as Grogu walked over to where the Jedi stood.

From behind Luke came a bright chirping noise as the blue-and-white astromech droid R2-D2 rolled in. Grogu and the droid faced each other, R2-D2 beeping and the Child cooing at him. Looking up, Luke met Mando's gaze.

The Child looked at Luke and raised his arms, and the Jedi lifted him.

"May the Force be with you," Luke said. He turned and walked out the door, with R2-D2 rolling along behind him.

His eyes shining with emotion, Mando watched them leave, Grogu gazing at him over Luke's shoulder. As they stepped into the elevator, the Mandalorian took one last look at the Child.

Then the doors closed, and they were gone.

EPILOGUE

NIGHT FELL FAST ON TATOOINE.

In the palace that had once belonged to Jabba the Hutt, Bib Fortuna sat holding court on the throne of the dead galactic crime lord. The Twi'lek had grown fat in his ascent to power, his jowls drooping along with the glistening lekku that wrapped around his neck and hung over his chest. Courtiers and various hangers-on formed his entourage. Gamorrean guards stood watch on either side, and a terrified Twi'lek captive was chained by her ankle to the base of the throne.

Bib sat back with a chortle, enjoying the spoils of his success. It was good to be king.

Then, from the stairwell above, there was a series of blaster flashes.

Bib leaned forward, commanding the guards in Huttese. The Gamorreans advanced toward the unseen altercation. Two more blaster shots rang out, and both guards fell to the floor, dead. Worried, Bib ordered another of his minions forward, and another. More blaster fire sprayed through the throne room as one by one each of them fell.

All that remained was Bib himself, and the chained Twi'lek at his side.

Out of the shadows, Fennec Shand slipped into view. Bib gaped at her in astonished silence. Fennec aimed the sniper rifle in the direction of the enslaved Twi'lek and pulled the trigger. The chain snapped.

The Twi'lek woman seemed relieved and confused at the same time. With a subtle move of her head, Fennec signaled that she was free to go. The Twi'lek leapt to her feet and ducked into the shadows with her newly gained freedom.

Fennec stood looking at Bib Fortuna. The crime boss was still staring at her when Boba Fett walked into the room, holding a blaster.

Bib gaped at his new guest. "Boba," he said in Huttese. "I thought you were dead." A queasy smile came over his face. "I am so glad to see you. I heard many rumors."

Boba pointed the blaster and fired. Bib jerked once and slumped forward.

Stepping onto the platform, Boba Fett shoved the lifeless body aside and settled himself into the seat of power. Next to him, Fennec uncapped a bottle of blue liquor and lifted it to her lips.

Seated on the throne, Boba Fett gazed out, his eyes directed toward the future.